DEADLY DNA

DEADLY DNA

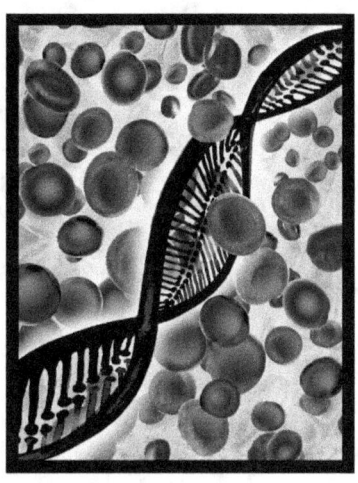

MIKE TRIAL

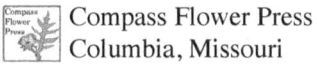
Compass Flower Press
Columbia, Missouri

Cover art by Yolanda Ciolli
Book design by Yolanda Ciolli

Published by
Compass Flower Press
Columbia, Missouri

Library of Congress Control Number: 2020920800
ISBN: 978-1-951960-12-4 Trade Paperback
ISBN: 978-1-951960-13-1 Ebook

Acknowledgments

My apologies to genetic researchers and engineers for treating gene editing in my story as an elixir able to make instantaneous changes in the human body and mind. I did this to speed the pace of the story. In real life, the processes of gene editing are much different —and more fascinating than any fictional depiction could be.

My thanks to the usual gang, Yolanda, and Geoff, and Theresa, for helping me bring Deadly DNA from idea to novella.

Chapter One

The invitation to the film school party said "dressy-cool," and since my boyfriend Rick's film was among the five finalists, I wanted to look extra-special good. Rick picked me up at my apartment, looking great in jeans, an open-collar ruffled-front tuxedo shirt, and a black sports jacket. "You look great!" I told him.

"And you look beautiful," he said.

I'm a little on the skinny side to wear the purple off-the-shoulder cocktail dress I'd bought for the party, but I'm curvy enough to fill it out. Black shoes, silver necklace and earrings, with my hair styled shorter and darker—I'll admit, I did think I looked pretty good.

He hit the accelerator of his Dodge Challenger hard, and we both laughed.

It was great to be alive.

The party was sponsored by the University of Iowa's Directorate of Research. It was to celebrate the completion of a set of short promotional videos the film school seniors had made to showcase the research UI was doing. The director of research, Dr. DeSteele herself, was going to be there to announce the winners. These short videos would be used to attract researchers and students to UI.

The place was crowded when we arrived. A string quartet labored to make itself heard over the happy noise of a throng of people dressed in everything from jeans and T-shirts to tuxedos and evening gowns. Before we'd even gotten our complimentary glasses of champagne, Rick pulled me through the crowd to where Dr. DeSteele stood surrounded by worshipful students.

"Dr. DeSteele, I'd like you to meet Francesca Mechlin," Rick said, beaming.

DeSteele turned her intense gaze on me. "Pleased to meet you," she told me with a politician's smile. She had charisma; I found it hard to take my eyes off of her. Her handshake was short and sharp. She was dressed very well in black slacks and a fire-engine-red jacket that complemented her coal-black hair.

"Francesca helped me with my film entry," Rick said with obvious pride. I found I liked being shown off. His hand felt good on my shoulder. "My film is the one featuring genetic engineering, which Francesca…"

Dr. DeSteele's expression changed subtly. "Yes, the genetic engineering film," she interrupted, taking Rick's elbow. "Mr. Page, I need for you to have a word with my assistant, if you don't mind." At a glance from DeSteele, her assistant materialized beside us and pulled Rick away. DeSteele's attention was already back on the others crowding around her.

Feeling a little abandoned, I made my way to the table where servers were pouring champagne. I got two glasses and found a place to wait for Rick.

It wasn't long until he arrived, scowling. I've always thought he looked a lot like Steve McQueen—great smile, great hair. But tonight his expression was so dark he looked like somebody else.

I handed him his champagne.

"I'm out!" he snapped, drinking down half his champagne.

"What?"

"You heard me," he snarled. He drank the rest of the champagne and looked around the room at the happy crowd. "DeSteele's assistant told me my film is being pulled out of the competition. I needed to get advance permission to film anything to do with genetic engineering. You should have told me your project is confidential!"

"It isn't," I stuttered. "I don't know...I've never heard of..."

Rick shook his head. "Yeah, I guess you don't know, do you?" He looked around again. "I need to talk to some people," he told me. "I'll see you later."

He stalked off through the crowd.

I couldn't hold back tears. I had no tissues with me, so I dabbed at my eyes with a cocktail napkin and bolted out into the cool night air. Down the sidewalk a bit I stopped to text my best friend Leah. *Can you come over and pick me up at the Arts and Science Building right now? Rick and I had an argument...I need a ride. I'll be at the end of the sidewalk by that Confucius Institute sign.*

Be there in ten minutes, Leah said. She's good about answering her texts.

A few minutes later Leah's white Sentra pulled up.

"What happened?" Leah said as we drove off. "By the way, you look great except for that mascara running down your face."

"This has been the worst night of my life," I said, dabbing at my face with the soggy cocktail napkin. "Rick's film has been disqualified. They just told him tonight."

"I thought he'd been notified it was one of the finalists."

"He was notified of that yesterday, but tonight it's been disqualified and he's blaming me."

"What! Why?"

"Well, I suggested the topic—the genetic engineering research I'm doing. He shot a bunch of footage in my lab in the Hathman Building…"

"I know all that," Leah interrupted. "I want to know about you and Rick."

"Well, we hadn't been at the party five minutes when Dr. DeSteele's assistant took Rick aside to tell him something. I wasn't part of the conversation, but apparently they disqualified his film because it showed some of the equipment in my genetics lab— my equipment."

"Gene splicers, that crispy critter stuff?"

I nodded.

"He did some establishing shots that showed all my labmate Susan's and my equipment."

"So?"

"I don't know. All I can think is that the CRISPR equipment Susan and I both use is the same as the ones they use up at the corporate research campus in Coralville. Maybe DeSteele thinks Rick's film shows too much, maybe hints at the patentable corporate stuff being done up at the Coralville Research Campus. I don't know."

I started crying again.

Leah stopped to wait for a university catering truck to back into the loading dock of Campus Food Services.

"Would you look at this idiot?" Leah gestured at the truck, which now had one rear wheel up on the curb and was spinning its other tires. It eased forward, angled, and tried backing in again. This time it made it.

"Idiot!" Leah snorted. The light at Parker Street had changed to red, so we had to sit and wait some more.

"Anyway," I continued. "Rick was in high spirits when we arrived, the happiest I've seen him in weeks… but now…"

"High spirits would be an improvement," Leah interrupted. "He's really seemed tense lately." She cast a glance at me. "You do too. I think both of you are working too hard."

"Anyway," I continued, "after DeSteele's assistant talked to Rick, he came back to me as angry as I've ever seen him. 'I'm out of the competition,' he said and stomped off to talk to people. Anybody but me."

The catering workers from the truck were now unloading glass holders, probably from the party I'd just come from.

"Hey, I've got an idea!" I told Leah. "Pull in beside that truck!"

"Are you crazy?" Leah said, but she pulled in to the loading dock beside the catering truck.

Nobody was around, so I picked up a plastic tray with twenty-four empty champagne glasses in it ready for the dishwasher. "Pop the trunk," I told Leah. I stowed the tray in the trunk of her car, got in, and we continued toward my apartment.

Leah raised an eyebrow at me. "You go from crying over Rick to stealing glassware? Does the word kleptomaniac mean anything to you? Or schizophrenia? You want to explain what you just did?"

"I need more DNA samples for my research baseline."

"I thought you were using volunteers to provide gum swabs."

"I am, but it's too slow. Students come in once in a while, and even though I give them $5 for two minutes of their time, I've only got two hundred samples. I need just a few more to build a minimally statistically significant baseline."

"Which will probably cost you a $100 fine for stealing university property."

"I'll return the glassware tomorrow."

"Well, at least it took your mind off Rick. He'll come back to you. He's a nice guy," Leah said in her mothering tone, then added briskly, "At risk of reopening the wound, I wonder why Dr. DeSteele considers genetic engineering such a touchy subject that she won't use Rick's promo video. I thought genetic engineering was one of the major initiatives of this university. Unlike stodgy old English literature." Leah did her pathetic look. "My grant is one tenth the size of yours. My office…well, you've heard my sob story before. If the university would get that ridiculous Confucius Institute out of the Arts and Science Building I might be able to get an office bigger than a broom closet."

"I didn't realize how big that institute is," I said. "The party tonight was in their auditorium, which is the whole end of the building." Remembering the party started my tears again.

Leah pulled up in the visitor drop-off at my apartment building.

I sat there a moment collecting myself. "I've never seen Rick so angry. I thought he was going to punch somebody—me, maybe."

"You two ought to cool off. You're both wound way too tight." I nodded and mopped up my tears with a tissue from the box in Leah's car. Leah touched my shoulder. "Give yourself some time. Give Rick some time."

"Time is what we don't have. The end of the semester is in three weeks. Rick will graduate and leave town… I've still got a year to go on my doctorate…"

My phone pinged. "It's a text from Rick," I told Leah. "He says he's sorry and wants to talk."

"Good," Leah said, back in mothering mode. "Tell him you'll meet him right now, someplace you both like. Tell him you're sorry…"

"I'm not sorry! It's not my fault…"

"You ARE sorry his film was disqualified, that's all. You're not saying you are responsible. But don't argue with him about who's right and who's wrong. Talk about how to make things better. Don't waste time you don't have."

I tried to think of what to say to Rick.

"Text him back, he's waiting," Leah said.

I texted him that I'd meet him at the Airliner bar, our favorite beer joint, in twenty minutes. It would be a good place to put things right. I felt better already.

"Okay Mother Leah, I'll take your advice," I said as I got out of the car. "Pop the trunk will you, so I can get that glassware."

"Fix your makeup," Leah called after me as I wrestled the tray of glasses out of the trunk. "You look like Vampirella."

I put the glassware in the trunk of my car, went up to my apartment and changed, and was at the Airliner right on time. Rick was there sitting at our usual booth, two glasses of beer already on the table. He looked calm, even gave me a small, rather contrite smile. I'd been telling myself on the drive over here that Rick was really a calm, centered kind of guy. Except for the blowup at the party tonight, I'd never seen him angry. I slid into the booth, took a sip of beer to steady my nerves, and launched into the speech I'd rehearsed.

"I am sorry your film wasn't previewed at the party, Rick; I'm really sorry about that. I should have checked with somebody in the research director's office to make sure it was okay to video in my lab. I didn't. It never occurred to me that anything we're doing should be kept secret." I paused, took another sip, and pressed ahead. "What can I do to see that your film gets back in the competition?" I took his hand and held it.

"It's all right, Fran. It's already fixed. After you left, DeSteele's assistant caught up with me again and told me the whole thing had been a mix-up. Her staff had assumed my video was shot at the Coralville Campus. When they found out it wasn't, everything was okay. They apologized and said my film had been reinstated in the competition. I finished third."

"That's great news," I breathed. *Still, there was something strange about the director of research herself being touchy about filming in my lab. Genetic engineering was supposed to be one of the university's strategic initiatives.*

Rick was staring at his beer. His smile had disappeared. "Yeah, my promo video may get selected, but it's my thesis video that counts." He looked at me with a look I couldn't read. Was he blaming me for convincing him to take the time to enter the promo video competition? He'd originally said he was too busy, but Leah and I had convinced him to take time to make the promo video. He really is a talented filmmaker.

"I'm behind schedule on my thesis film, and tonight at the party, Sherry Alton, my assistant editor, says she's quitting my project. Says she has to concentrate on her finals." The anger in his tone scared me a little. "I need her to finish the job she agreed to, not quit at the last minute. And especially not with some phony excuse."

"You've still got three days, right?"

"Yeah, three days."

The PA was softly playing an old Johnny Rivers song that under other circumstances would have brought a smile to both our faces. I still hoped Rick would talk out his anger tonight and we could get back on track with each other. My project was behind schedule too. We needed each other to be supportive, not use up time neither one of us had blaming each other.

"How can I help?" I asked.

"You can't," he said bluntly. "Unless you can run an ARRI video editor. I've got no assistant editor, and 20 percent of the editing still to be done."

"Yes," I said as sympathetically as I could.

Rick quit squinting at his beer, took a solid slug of it, and breathed a great sigh. "I'll have to do the rest of the editing myself." After a moment's silence, he looked around the empty bar, frowned, sighed another sigh, and started turning his glass in quarter circles. "I…I need to talk about something with you, Fran."

My blood froze.

He kept turning his beer glass in little quarter circles, not meeting my eye. "I think…I know…we're both under schedule pressure. I think that pressure is making us both feel bad. I know I don't feel my best tonight, and maybe now is not the right time to talk about this. It's probably just the stress of getting my film finished. I can do it, but…I can't deal with distractions right now. Anyway…" He stopped talking, looked at his glass, at the nearly empty bar, at the bartender, everywhere but at me.

I found I was holding my breath and quietly let it out.

"What I'm saying, Fran, is that I think, until graduation, we shouldn't see each other." He took my hand. "It's not about you, it's about me. I've got to get my film done even if I have to work 24/7…I've got to get it done."

And once it's done, you'll graduate, I said to myself. *And then what happens to us? You're not going to hang around Iowa City another year waiting for me to finish up my doctorate. You're going to go someplace where you can get involved with the indie film scene…while I'm still back here slogging away in the lab. Might as well just say goodbye now.*

I squeezed his hand and nodded okay, hoping he didn't see the tears in my eyes. "I understand," I managed to say.

"Sorry," he said. He stood and pulled cash out of his jeans and laid it on the table. "We'll get past this, Fran. I know we will, but right now, I've got to focus…"

"It's okay, Rick," I told him. I linked arms with him as we strolled out into a mild summer night.

When we got to his car, he gave me a quick kiss on the cheek, then got in and drove away, leaving me standing alone in the soft night breeze.

A tear trickled down my right cheek and I wiped it off with the back of my hand. I walked to my car and got in, telling myself: *Once he graduates, and the pressure is off, we'll figure out what comes next. It will all work out.*

I tried to smile at myself in the rearview mirror, but my smile slid away and I sat there crying.

Chapter Two

I dried my tears. Sitting in my car moping over Rick was not helping me get my project back on schedule. I was still upset over today's events, and I knew I couldn't sleep, so I drove to campus.

That's what I always do in times of emotional stress—bury myself in work.

It was late, but I often work late, although I liked it better a year ago when there were other people in the building. These days the Hathman Building feels a little spooky late at night since all the labs on the lower level are empty except for mine, which I share with my labmate Susan. Over the course of the last year all the other researchers have moved up to the newer lab facilities at the Coralville Campus.

The front entrance of the Hathman is well lighted, though I've never trusted the hedges the university insists on having on either side of the entrance. I hurriedly swiped my card through the reader, pushed inside, and cycled the airlock. The Hathman Building had a negative-pressure air system installed several years ago when the former chemistry labs were refitted for genetic engineering research.

The corridor lights were always on. I went downstairs and swiped my card in the reader at my lab door. Inside, I heaved a sigh, sat down at my desk, and got the software running. The clock in the computer said it was 11:30 PM.

An hour later I had gone through my sample database thoroughly. All samples were sequenced and checked for sampling errors. No errors. But the software that fits the curve could not a get a fit within the 99.9 percent I needed to find the right part of the DNA strand to do my edit.

I needed the curve smooth enough to show I had a credible baseline of unedited DNA samples, but spiky enough in the areas where my edit would occur so that my editor could find exactly the right spot.

I increased the scale on the vertical axis to make all the various splice points more apparent. The spikes were there, but there was still too much scatter to clearly define the exact point where the cutter enzyme would insert itself into the DNA strand.

I slumped in my chair. I had already spent three months persuading student volunteers to drop by and let me take a gum swab. It was painless and took about two minutes, but nobody wanted to do it. Two months ago I'd taken $500 out of the fast-dwindling miscellaneous expenses account in my grant funding, set up a table in the Arts and Science Building, and offered student volunteers $5 each for a sample. That had gotten me my second hundred samples. But still the baseline curve was not good enough. And my next six-month progress report to my thesis committee was due in a week.

The tray of champagne glasses I'd "borrowed" from Campus Catering was sitting on the counter. That would give me twenty-four more data points. But it was now midnight, and I was too exhausted to do the tedious work of sample prep and analysis.

Instead I wrote out a paragraph describing my curve fit attempt, saved the Excel curve and paragraph, and closed my laptop. Time to go home and get a good night's sleep, then bring in the glasses and get back to it fresh in the morning. In the last hour and a half I hadn't thought about Rick once. That, at least, was good.

It was then that the soft sounds I'd been hearing registered. Footsteps out in the corridor, and not those of someone purposefully walking by, but more like someone furtively creeping along. The indicator light on my lab door was red—locked. Only someone with a key to this lab could get in here, so I should be safe.

But who would be creeping around the corridor at this time of night?

Only my labmate Susan and I had key cards that would open the lab door. But who might have access to the building, I didn't know. Campus Security would have access, and probably the cleaning contractor, maybe others.

The sounds stopped. I started to call out "Susan?" but didn't. I stayed absolutely silent.

After a moment it sounded like the footsteps went back down the corridor toward the exit. *Should I open the door and see who it was? No, better to let them leave, which it sounded like they were doing, then get out of here fast.*

After the sounds faded I eased my door open. The corridor was empty. I grabbed my laptop, pulled my lab door silently closed, and crept down the corridor to the stairs, then paused listening. There was no sound except the whisper of the air system.

I tiptoed up the stairs to the building's front door, which consisted of two sets of sliding glass doors—one set of which had to close before the other would open. There was no one in sight. Outside, the parking lot was empty except for my car. But who knows who might be hiding in the hedges along the front of the building, and my car was a hundred feet away. My heart was pounding. I stood against the wall and texted Leah, *Are you sleeping or are you up and about?*

She texted me back immediately. *I just finished my final report on seventeenth century lit and I'm feeling pretty good. Let's go get a glass of wine, or is it past your bedtime?*

I told her: *It is past my bedtime, but a glass of wine sounds good. I'm just leaving the lab. I'll meet you at the Airliner in fifteen minutes.* I took a deep breath, sprinted to my car, and drove straight to the Airliner. Inside, the soft light and the familiar smell of beer dissipated my paranoia.

Leah was in the last booth on the right. "You still look distraught," Leah said. "Two Alexander Valley Cabernets please," she told the waiter.

"Just jittery," I said as I slid into the booth. "My lab is a pretty spooky building at night."

Our wines came. This is another feature I like about the Airliner—the service is lightning fast. Leah and I toasted each other and sipped.

Before she could say anything, I told her, "Don't counsel me about Rick, okay? We had a talk; we're working things out. He's not mad about his film; in fact that was all a misunderstanding. But we've agreed not to see each other until he's got his thesis film done." I flashed her the best smile I could muster. "Why are you rolling your eyes?"

"I'm your best friend so I can say this without you taking it the wrong way."

"I don't like it already," I said.

"Maybe you two should stop seeing each other right now. He's going to graduate in a week. He'll doubtless want to work someplace that has a film community, maybe LA. It certainly won't be Iowa City. Trying to maintain your relationship after he graduates…I just don't think it could work."

"Okay, okay, that's logical," I said, my anger rising. "But I'm going to wait a few days to make that decision. I said I don't want to talk about it, okay?" I just realized why my stomach was growling—I hadn't eaten anything since lunch. "I'm starving. I'm going to order a salad."

Leah nodded. "Good. You eat while I read you some of my paper, which I just happen to have right here on my phone."

I ordered a Cajun chicken salad with blue cheese dressing on the side.

Leah pulled her paper up on her phone. "Okay, while you stuff your face, I'll educate you on an interesting facet of fourteenth-century Europe…"

"That assumes there is an interesting facet," I mumbled around a mouthful of lettuce.

"Shut up and listen…the Black Death that decimated Europe in the fourteenth century spread far faster than could reasonably be expected to happen if the disease vector was exclusively flea-ridden black rats…"

"This is not great dinnertime conversation."

Leah continued. "…which was the accepted theory, although the rat vector was at odds with the extremely fast spread of the disease. A few years ago a researcher hypothesized that the Black Death was actually two diseases. One was plague, caused by infected fleas on rats, the other was anthrax, transmitted from infected cattle to humans." Leah smiled at this grim bit of history. "It all makes sense, cattle carrying anthrax could quickly spread the infection through every cattle market on the continent and across the channel to England."

She read on for a few more moments about how cattle anthrax worked in tandem with plague bacteria. After finishing my salad I was suddenly overcome with fatigue. I couldn't concentrate on what Leah was saying. I found myself staring at her hand on her wineglass, which she was absentmindedly turning in small circles as she read from her phone. I remembered Rick's strong, beautiful hands turning his beer glass in quarter circles, and I began to tear up.

Leah saw the tears in my eyes. "You don't need to become so concerned. The Black Death ended six hundred years ago." She put her phone away.

I mopped my eyes with my napkin. "I'm just tired."

"You are way past being tired, Fran—you're exhausted. Go home. Get some sleep."

I nodded. "You're right…"

"And text me when you get home so I'll know the bogeyman didn't get you."

When I got to my apartment, I went through every room to make sure no one was hiding there, chiding myself for feeling so paranoid. I dutifully texted Leah, then slipped off my clothes and was asleep the moment I laid down. But my dreams were not pleasant: dark figures creeping by my door, data sets that I couldn't interpret, and a nightmare in which my deplaquer genetic edit had been improperly formulated. Instead of helping people, it was killing them. They lay all about me, dying, with symptoms that looked like the Black Death.

That was the worst one.

The next morning I stopped by River Styx, the indie coffee shop with the best coffee in town, got a double mind-blaster so full of caffeine it would bring the dead back to life, then went to my lab.

Susan was not there yet. We were put together in this shared lab since my project uses findings from her project, which she has just about completed. She's a nice-looking girl from a small town, quiet and competent. The only conversations we've ever had have been about our projects. I got up to stand looking at the photo of Susan and the overweight guy she's engaged to back home. Then I went back to my desk and got the analytics program running, recleaned the sampler, and started getting DNA samples from the glassware I'd borrowed after the party last night. It was tedious work preparing samples—I had to take three swipes from the rim of each glass, run each one through the sequencer, then put that glass back in the tray and on to the next one. Ten minutes per glass.

It was silent in the lab except for the discreet whisper of the air containment and cleaning system. Visitors aren't encouraged to come to the Hathman Building. Not because anything we're doing is secret, but just because the fewer times the air control system has to cycle people in and out, the better.

But it makes it a bit lonely, working all day without friends dropping by just to chat. Leah has mentioned more than once that I stand a good chance of becoming a recluse working in this lab. Was that causing me to cling too tightly to Rick? I put Rick out of my mind and concentrated on getting my samples sequenced. Despite the coffee, I felt really lethargic this morning. I had to struggle to stay on task.

But for the first time in a month I felt like I was making progress. Finally I had enough random DNA samples for the testing phase of my project. I've had my gene editor designed since last September, and now I am doing the analytics to see if it works in computer modeling. After that comes animal testing, then clinical trials on humans. People suffer strokes when bits of plaque that have built up on capillary walls (usually due to eating too much cholesterol-laden food) break free and clog a capillary. Since blood is not flowing through the clogged capillary, the cells near it are getting no oxygen. When those cells are in the brain, damage starts to occur within minutes; permanent debility or death often results. My gene edit will continuously keep plaque dissolved in the blood so that blood phages can break it down and plaque will never build up.

I have my gene designed, mostly, and I have the clipper enzyme. Susan's genetic modulator will be an elegant little part of my design, providing negative feedback on the deplaquing so that if there is plaque on capillary walls, my edit won't dissolve it so fast it will overwhelm the phages that get rid of it. Without the modulator, the deplaquer would quickly dissolve a massive amount of plaque, which could easily block a capillary, which would cause a stroke.

With the modulator, my deplaquer is entirely safe, but without the modulator my deplaquer would be very dangerous for most people, since most people have some plaque coating their capillaries.

I will be using an off-the-shelf clipper enzyme, which is the part of the system that gets through a cell membrane. Two months ago I bought 10 cc of the enzyme, which will be my helix strand clipper. I had the precious stuff in the locked refrigerator here in the lab.

Once my deplaquer, with modulator attached, is ready for animal testing, it will be administered intravenously to assure the dosage is correct.

I worked steadily until the clock on my computer showed me it was past noon and I was starting to get really hungry. Coffee is not breakfast. But I stayed at it until I had all twenty-four glasses sampled and the data filed and backed up.

I shut down the sequencer and stood up, creaking. *I'll go get a quick sandwich at the Campus Shoppes, then a long, leisurely, mind-clearing walk around the quad in the shade of the big oaks.*

I heard footsteps in the corridor, and my heart froze. Then there was the click of the card reader unlocking the lab door, and in walked Susan.

I relaxed. "Hi Susan," I said cheerily. She mumbled a hello. She did not look happy.

"I think I'm making progress," I told her. "Still trying to get my sample data curve-fit, but I'll get it done eventually. But I can add your modulator to my theoretical design and start running simulations…"

She wasn't paying attention. She had put a floppy Campus Shoppes bag on her desk and was filling it with stuff from her desk drawers.

"So I'd like to get your modulator design sometime soon if you don't mind," I repeated.

She nodded okay and continued clearing out her desk. She carefully set her little brass nameplate reading

"Susan Allison" in the bag. I'd always thought that was silly having her nameplate on her desk when nobody ever came down here to our lab. The last person who had visited the lab was the technician from Fujitsu I'd called to fix the sample analyzing machine, and that was a year ago.

"Going somewhere?" I ventured.

She stopped to stare at the modest engagement ring on her left hand. "I'm leaving," she said.

"Leaving?" I knew she only had a final rewrite on her thesis plus her oral thesis defense before she would have her doctorate. Maybe three weeks of work.

She continued putting her things in the bag. "Charles and I have decided to get married right away."

I stared at her a few seconds. "I thought you were planning on a fall wedding and a honeymoon on a cruise ship."

"We changed our minds." She picked up the kitschy little framed photo of her fiancé, looked at it for a moment, then put it in the bag. "We probably won't take a honeymoon right away," she went on in a monotone. "I need to find a job…" She started twisting her engagement ring.

My jaw dropped. "Are you serious? You're quitting your project entirely, dropping out of the university? All you have left to do is a final rewrite of your thesis, then the oral defense. Maybe three or four weeks' work?"

She looked at me with sad eyes. "My grant has been terminated. Dr. DeSteele herself called me in last week and broke the news." She tried a smile that didn't work. "She told me I needed to move my research to the Coralville Campus, and I told her I only had two or three weeks of work to do to complete my degree requirements, but she said I had to move now." Susan stood by her desk, shoulders bowed.

"Why not take a month off, then come back to the Coralville Campus, complete your thesis, and schedule your oral defense. Once that's over you've got your degree and can leave UI."

She shook her head. "I'm not sure I want to be a genetic engineer anymore. And you and I have talked before about the restrictions up at the Coralville Campus that would make the isolation even worse than here."

She was on the verge of tears.

I stood up and moved toward her, but I've never really been a huggy person, so I just sort of stood near her, trying to project sympathy. "Don't give up now. You're so close…"

"No. I think I'm done with genetic engineering." She stopped twisting her ring and looked at the green Campus Shoppes bag.

I was horrified to see tears starting to run down Susan's pale cheeks.

"Sorry," Susan said, pulling herself together. "I'll be

fine. I'll go back to Worthington, Charles and I will get married, then I'll start thinking about what I really want to do."

"That's not what you used to say," I told her. "You used to be just as enthusiastic as I am about gene editing and the health benefits…anyway, there's nothing…" I stopped before I told her she probably wouldn't enjoy being a waitress in Worthington, Minnesota, the rest of her life. "Don't quit. Go back home, get married, take your honeymoon; then come back. Even if you have to work at Coralville, it's better than not finishing your degree." I was babbling, so stopped myself. She wasn't listening anyway.

Susan looked at me. "My leaving won't impact your project. My design of the modulator is done." Susan handed me a blue terabyte external drive. "Here's the design and a full set of the data I used for the design." She tilted her head at her desktop computer. "Some of my files are there on that computer, but they aren't organized and I just don't feel like taking the time to organize them."

"Thank you, Susan," I said, and awkwardly hugged her. She gave me a wan smile and picked up her bag of stuff. I opened the lab door for her and watched her trudge down the corridor and up the stairs.

I'd never really gotten to know Susan in the year I'd shared this lab with her, but she had always been cheerful, and exuberant about genetic engineering, just like me. And now I never would get to know her. Leah is right. I need to be more in contact with people or I'm going to become a recluse.

I grabbed a bite of lunch then slogged through the afternoon collating data from the twenty-four samples from the borrowed glassware. By 4 PM I had the data collated and now my curve-fit was worse, not better.

The way the curve-fitting algorithms work is that the more data points you have, the better the curve fits the data points, assuming the data has a commonality in the section of the DNA helix that you are interested in. And unedited human DNA should be virtually identical in the area I was looking at, which would give me a baseline curve to help me select exactly where the cut point should be.

But with the glassware samples, my curve was worse than it had been without them. "This can't be right," I muttered. I was beginning to get a headache but forced myself to continue.

I checked the sampling procedure, which has a built-in recording of the steps and results from sample analysis. Each of the twenty-four samples was done correctly. I sat there staring at my computer screen.

I felt bad. Not just about Susan, not just about Rick and me, but just plain bad—my head ached and I was dead tired. And now I had data points to analyze, which would cost me a day or two, my project was already behind schedule, and I had my end-of-semester progress report due.

I felt overwhelmed. I shut down my computers, dropped Susan's external drive into my purse, collected my laptop, and lugged the tray of glassware up the stairs, out the airlock, and to my car. I told myself that once I dropped off the glassware at Campus Catering and went home, I would start working on integrating Susan's modulator into my deplaquer.

But I could not force myself to do any of this. Instead I drove straight home and went to bed.

Chapter Three

The next morning, still not feeling well, I dragged myself out of bed and drove to Campus Catering. Two local louts were sitting on the loading dock smoking cigarettes.

"Got some glassware that ended up in my car by mistake," I said cheerily to the one with the black beard stubble and some truly hideous tattoos on his forearms. He grinned, flipped his cigarette away, and sauntered over.

I popped the trunk and hopped out.

"Must of been a pretty good party, honey," he leered as he hoisted the tray out.

His buddy sitting on the loading dock laughed. "Yeah, next time you either invite us or we're turning you in to the campus cops for stealing university property.

I closed the trunk and drove off.

I drove up Dubuque Avenue until I found an Applebee's. While I worked my way through the breakfast special, I looked through back files of the CRISPR users' group proceedings on my laptop.

A word search found me a paper from about a year ago where researchers at Cornell had identified a gene splice that seemed to correlate well with correcting anti-herd behavior in herd animals, like goats. It worked by realigning a gene that controlled hormonal secretions, a place on the DNA helix very close to where Susan had located her modulator. I could use the Cornell data to help me design how to fit the modulator to my deplaquer.

They'd even done some field testing at the animal sciences research farm here at UI. The appendix had the basic coding. It looked very similar to what I needed to integrate Susan's modulator to my deplaquer, but I couldn't be sure until I got back to the lab and actually ran some detailed analyses. I copied the coding sequence to a new file and closed my computer.

"Anything more, ma'am?" the young black waiter asked me cheerfully.

"Did you know that a goat's herd instinct overrides even hunger or thirst?" I told him. "A thirsty goat will stay with its herd even if water is not far away. It will wait until the whole herd moves to the water."

He grinned. "That's good to know. And speaking of thirsty, would you like more coffee? Or something sweet?" He slid a glossy menu with thousand-calorie treats toward me, but I pushed it away. Which took some effort. When I don't feel well, I tend to eat a lot—mostly sweets.

"No thanks, just the check." It spooled out of the card reader on his belt, and he laid it on the table.

"Thanks for your goat info," he laughed. "I'm a music major, but I may need to take up goat herding someday to pay the bills."

I laid a twenty on the bill and drove back to my lab. Then I sat in the car for five minutes wishing I could take the day off, go home, and lie around all day doing nothing.

But I didn't. I dutifully went inside and downstairs to my lab, got my programs running, and worked for an hour designing an integration based on the Cornell design. That went pretty well.

But after a while my thoughts drifted to the sunny day outside and me in my cold, silent cell, working away, lonely and not feeling very well.

Last fall, not long after I'd met Rick, we rented bicycles and rode out to Harland Park for a picnic. Back then everything seemed good. Rick was wonderful, I didn't feel pressured to get my project back on schedule, my life seemed perfect. But now...

I set the integration design aside and studied my data set again. I needed it to fit to within 99.9 percent, and it was down around 90 percent. I tried an entirely new algorithm that, after an hour's effort, didn't make the data fit any better.

I sat there for a while feeling sorry for myself. Then I got up and paced and gave myself my usual pep talk. *If I can get my system to work, the health benefits will be momentous. The gains to medicine and health are worth the time invested, my time, in months of analysis, searching up blind alleys, and failed testing. If I can stop capillary plaque from flaking off into the bloodstream, it will eliminate strokes. And in fact, my system will allow patients to prevent plaque from building up on capillary walls in the first place. People will be safe from strokes, no matter how bad their diet. People can eat those giant Applebee's fudge sundaes every day if they want.*

I felt like eating one now. The building was cold and ominously silent except for the soft sound of the air system. I looked at the clock on the computer screen: 6:30 already.

I glanced at Susan's empty desk. It seemed so strange that she was gone. I'd taken her presence for granted. She may have been quiet, but she was very competent and we were comfortable sharing the lab. We had seldom talked of anything except our two projects and how they fit together.

I felt through my purse for the external drive she'd given me. It was there. *Why had she been so passive about her grant cancellation? Using it as an excuse to quit the university. A strange time to quit and go get married when you are a few weeks away from getting your doctorate. Choosing to be a housewife instead of a researcher in a field that had nearly unlimited possibilities for improving human life. I guess I really didn't know her at all.*

I'd been staring at her desk for a full minute before I realized her desktop computer was gone. I opened a desk drawer. Susan had taken her personal stuff, but she'd left the usual collection of pens, pencils, and paper. But now everything was gone.

Over the smooth whisper of the air recycler I heard slow, almost furtive steps, as though someone was coming down the hall not sure what door they were looking for. As they reached my door they resumed a normal pace and faded down the hallway.

My phone pinged. It was Leah. *It's happy hour. You're late.*

On my way, I texted back. I closed my laptop, opened the lab door a crack to see that the corridor was empty, then hurried outside. It was a delicious late-spring evening.

Twenty minutes later I was seated across from Leah in our usual booth. I always feel better in the Airliner. It was surprisingly full this Wednesday evening. For dinner we both had the so-called 'Airliner special' (ordinary hamburger and fries), which is still as bad as when I first came to UI. I don't know why I keep ordering it. But the beer is always good. There's a local brewery that produces a great IPA.

As we ate I whined to Leah about data I couldn't interpret, about Susan leaving, about Rick and me not being together, about me being sick and tired of all this stuff.

Leah looked at her empty plate. "You certainly aren't your usual upbeat self."

For some reason her tone struck me wrong. I sulked.

"Too many hours hunched monk-like over your computer in that dungeon you call a lab," Leah said. This irritated me even more. I needed useful advice, not criticism.

I sighed. "Well, I think my work is important. Here's what I spent the afternoon doing." I told her about the Cornell research. "I have enough samples now to make a good base data set, but it is not working. Using any standard algorithm, I should get a nice tight curve. I've tried several and none of them work. I used the algorithm the Cornell people used, and it still doesn't work. I spent all afternoon going up a blind alley..."

"Blind alleys are part of research," Leah said. "If you knew which alley to go up, it wouldn't be research."

I shook my head. "You don't understand. It's not a blind alley, it's just that the data defies proper interpretation. I know I'm doing the sample processing and data analysis right, but the results make no sense. I'm worn out."

"And you're wearing me out with all this negativity," Leah said.

I gave her a look and sipped my beer, hoping my irritation would subside. "I rechecked all my samples, including the party glassware, and there is no indication of a bad sample."

"Ah yes, the stolen glassware," Leah mused. "I'm expecting a rap on my door any day now by the campus cops looking for the getaway driver in the infamous glassware heist…"

"Don't joke about that, okay?" I snapped. "That joke has worn thin." I ignored her hurt look. "I returned the glassware to Campus Catering this morning."

Leah looked everywhere except at me.

I wanted her reassurance, but everything I was saying seemed wrong. Her upbeat personality was not there this evening, or maybe it was just me. She's a dual major—English literature and history. We've known each other since we were kids growing up in Lakeshore. I'm two years older than she is, but she always seemed like a big sister to me. I think she likes that role. And I like her, usually. I used to think it was because we were both passionate about what we are studying. Here at UI, we've fallen into the habit of getting together a couple of times a week; I patiently listen to her discussions of obscure, long-dead authors, and she listens to me enthuse about genetic engineering.

But tonight she was getting on my nerves.

"Sorry," I told Leah. "I'm really tired. I've been working my data for hours and hours and can't get it to fit. Those twenty-four samples from the party glassware skew the curve even worse. I've added every sample I have to the data set, even one I got from Rick a week ago."

Leah grinned, cheerful again. "A sample from Rick. Very interesting." She pointed at my face. "You're blushing! I can envision the scene now: in the midst of a torrid bedroom encounter, you suddenly run a sterile swab across Rick's gum, then dash to the bathroom and put the swab in a sealed container. If I had been Rick, I would have left your apartment then and there."

I tried to laugh, but I felt too tired to even laugh.

Leah changed the subject, reciting some anecdote from her paper on the fusion of story, drama, and early opera, something about Monteverdi, an early opera composer. My mind drifted. I couldn't focus on that stuff right now. All I could think about was why my data wouldn't organize and what I was going to do to get it to.

I realized Leah had stopped talking. "I'm boring you," she said flatly.

Leah finished her beer and slid out of the booth. "Well, I've got to be going." Her tone was just short of being huffy.

I waved, and she left.

I stared at her empty beer glass for a while, finished my beer, and got up to leave. At the last minute, without really thinking about it, I picked up Leah's glass, wrapped it in a paper napkin, and put it in my purse. *One more data point,* I told myself, knowing that was not the truth. I felt unwell, but that was no excuse for stealing glassware.

Chapter Four

I woke from a restless sleep feeling sorry for myself. The clock said 2 AM. The general malaise I'd been feeling lately was making me tired, but at the same time keeping me from sleeping well.

I got up and opened my laptop. My solution to not feeling well is always the same—immerse myself in work until I'm so exhausted I can sleep. Yesterday I'd told myself I'd set my misbehaving data set aside for a while and work on the integration of Susan's modulator into my gene editor, but as soon as I opened my laptop, I went straight back to the data set.

I could invest in some very sophisticated algorithms for analyzing data, but my project budget would not tolerate that, and besides, from what I'd read about them, they are so hard to operate you end up having to contract with the vendor to do the analysis. And it would take a lot of my fast-dwindling grant money, and several months, and I might end up with something I couldn't use.

I reran two separate, simpler algorithms, but both showed my data points would not fit the expected curve closer than 93 percent. Which was not good enough.

I stared at my screen. Then ran back through the analysis of my data. Then I sat there staring at my screen. My apartment was dead silent. No cars passed on the street outside. I couldn't think of anything that might resolve this impasse, so I said out loud, "Okay, set this aside and complete the integration design of Susan's modulator into my deplaquer."

The first step was to find the molecular arrangement where the editing enzymes would connect. Susan's data was neatly arranged, so it didn't take me long to have both molecular arrangements up on the screen.

There was something familiar about the modulator's molecular arrangement. I realized it was similar to the molecular arrangement of the enzyme the Cornell researchers used in their herd-behavior project.

I put my deplaquer information aside and put the herd-behavior and Susan's modulator up on my screen side by side. They were not identical, but very similar. Only a few of the forty link-points differed. A strange coincidence. As I looked at the two molecular arrangements, I realized Susan's modulator by itself, not connected to my deplaquer, would re-edit the herd-behavior edit developed by the Cornell researchers. It would reverse its effect, and presumably if administered to goats that had normal herd behavior, it would turn them into anti-social outcasts.

I laughed. "It's 3 AM and I've discovered how to make goats anti-social! Nobel prize, here I come!"

Laughing felt good. I worked partway through the design for linking the modulator to the deplaquer and got up to go to bed. But at the bedroom door I changed my mind and went back to my laptop.

I noticed the Cornell researchers had used a fairly small sample set (I guess anti-social goats are rare), so I decided to see what happened to my curve-fit by eliminating outliers—not usually a good idea, especially since almost 10 percent of my data points were outliers. But at this point I was willing to try anything.

With the outlying data points deleted from the data set, my curve-fit suddenly jumped up to 99 percent accurate.

So what is wrong with the outliers? I scanned back to find out which samples didn't fit, and after a few minutes had them all identified. They were the twenty-four samples from party glassware, plus Susan's sample from last week, and a sample of mine I'd taken yesterday. I labeled it the "cull" data set.

I took the cull data set, ran a backward pass to see how an edit might be performed on them, and got no results. I tried to step-analyze each chemical reaction, but got bogged down.

But when I sat back and thought about the data, I realized the cull data looked like an edit had already been done, almost. But not a full edit, a half edit.

"What is going on here?" I muttered and got up to pace.

The Cornell fix for anti-social behavior in herd animals and Susan's modulator were similar in design. Both the Cornell hormonal rebalance and my deplaquer with Susan's modulator involve two steps. The first step is to clip a DNA strand at a specific point and insert edited DNA. The second step is to clip out a segment of unedited DNA that is parallel with the inserted segment, then let the DNA strand heal itself by copying the new DNA, not the excised DNA. Then you have the full edit, which immediately goes to work producing the change that's wanted.

But if the edit is only half done, the DNA strand copies itself, but the copy doesn't match the insert. This does not produce the desired results.

My cull data samples were not similar to my deplaquer, but they were similar to Susan's modulator, which was similar to the edit the Cornell people had developed. I checked the Cornell research report, which was nicely written. I made a mental note to use it as a template for my own research report. They had conscientiously tested half edits, incorrect strand placement, inverted sequences—all the things you want to avoid when synthesizing an editor. They had been thorough. I also found that they had conducted field tests with incorrectly prepared edits. In those tests, the goats' hormonal systems went increasingly out of balance; the goats became over-social, obsessive followers, even to the point of not properly feeding.

The Cornell paper emphasized that care must be taken to get the edit right. An improper edit could cause major problems.

Fatigue was settling over me. It was time to try to sleep again. I lay back on the sofa and tried to clear my mind of everything, but I found myself instead remembering back in my Freshman year when Leah and I had come to spend a few days at my parents' house, and my father had insisted all of us go to an opera. My parents are opera buffs. Opera fanatics would be a better term. Anyway, while my mother was getting Leah settled in the guest bedroom, I tried to lay down the law to my father about how Leah and I wanted to go our own way—we had plenty of things in mind to do—but that fell on deaf ears. His response was that he had already bought our tickets to the Lyric Opera in downtown Chicago, and he insisted we all attend. "It's *La Bohème*. Everybody likes that one."

I was afraid that subjecting Leah to a three-and-a-half-hour opera the first night would completely destroy our friendship, but she not only put up with it, she liked it. Which was not hard to do—the soprano singing the Musetta role was wonderful. On the way home, Leah and I were in the back seat of the car singing "Musetta's Waltz" in harmony (kind of) until my mother finally turned around and said, "For heaven's sake, Francesca, be quiet. Your father can't concentrate on his driving with your racket."

We shut up. I saw my father's eyes smiling at us in the rearview mirror. "I'm pleased you like the opera, but I would suggest you not drop your genetic engineering studies and take up professional singing."

Despite the afternoon at the opera, Leah and I are still the best of friends.

In the past I have always envied her humor and her easy self-confidence. Why had it been getting on my nerves lately? "That's not like me," I said out loud. *I guess I am spending too much time alone in my lab. I don't have a life anymore.*

I got up, turned off the lights, and went to bed. To keep my mind on positive thoughts, I visualized the day my research was complete, my thesis published, my patents secured. I imagined myself accepting calls from the big drug manufacturers offering me loads of money for licensing rights to my design. I'm well aware that even if a new drug is worth millions of dollars, the inventor is normally only paid a 15 to 20 percent royalty, but that sure beats living on my current grad student stipend. I would become the next Rachel Haurwitz, the thirty-four-year-old genetic engineering researcher who perfected a genetic anticancer treatment, then found investors, started up her own company—Caribou Biosciences—and is now worth many millions of dollars.

I was almost asleep when my mind began to sift the facts in my research data again. My samples indicated a number of people had been administered a half gene edit, for some unknown reason. I was at the party, so I must have been administered the gene edit since my recent sample, taken after the party, was different from my older sample, taken before the party. My mind drifted into dark thoughts. *Who is administering half edits? And why? What results will it produce? How can it be reversed?* I tried to reassure myself that ingestion was a very poor method of administering a gene editor, so it was unlikely I would be affected.

Exhaustion eventually gave me a few hours of fitful sleep. I dragged myself out of bed at 7 AM, started slugging down coffee, and mentally prepared myself for another frustrating day at the lab.

Chapter Five

My phone pinged with a text as I was pulling into my parking place at the Hathman Building. *The director of research requests a short meeting with you this morning at 10 AM, room 2030, Coralville Administration Building. Please confirm if you are available.* I waited until I was downstairs in my lab before answering.

Susan had said she was called to the director's office last week to be told in person that she needed to move to Coralville. She hesitated, and her grant was terminated.

I sat in my chair shaking my head. *If I don't move, they might cancel my grant, which means I'll have to find alternate funding to complete my research. That will take me months of grant proposal writing and submitting, and while I'm doing that, they'll take my lab privileges away and move all my equipment to Coralville.*

"It's hopeless," I sighed. *But it would do no good to ignore the message. They know where I am and what I'm doing, so I might as well go see them and get the bad news in person.* I touched "accept appointment" on my phone.

I felt a tear leak out of my eye. It was not like me to feel so depressed. I used to have enough energy to look for alternate paths forward, but now, I just felt like giving up. *Why not just accept the inevitable—move to Coralville and let them run my project and control the dissemination of my results? Or I could leave UI, go to grad school somewhere else.*

If I'm forced to move, the best thing would be to have my design done and a prototype synthesized. Maybe I could stall DeSteele until the end of summer semester. I will have done the simulator testing of the prototype, synthesized a sample, designed my animal test program.

With a heavy heart I started my computer and brought my design up on the screen in both the graphical and the analytical views. The analytical description is the one that counts: it is lines of computer code interspersed with mathematical functions which describe the sequence of biochemical reactions the editor goes through to cut and reseal a DNA strand. The graphical depiction is a series of color 3D models representing the enzyme and the DNA strand clipping and insertion. It's useful for visualizing and useful for presentations, but you need the analytics to work with it.

I could barely force myself to work through my checklist of reactions, but I kept going and completed it. I decided to synthesize some deplaquer without the modulator now, in case I had to change labs. I knew it wasn't logical to synthesize a prototype this soon, but if I had to move and lose weeks in the move, I might as well get as far along as I could while I still had the freedom to do what I wanted.

I got my precious 12 cc of synthetic enzyme (which had cost $2,500) out of the refrigerator, measured out 3 cc, and put the rest away.

I put the enzyme in the airbox along with my tools and the reagents I'd need, then let the airbox pull the internal pressure down so anything in the atmosphere in the airbox would get pulled into the filters, not released into the lab. Then I slipped my hands into the gloves and went to work.

It took about ten minutes. The hard part is the design, not the synthesis.

When I was done, I had 3 cc of a clear fluid in a glass pipette. I pulled my hands out of the gloves and looked around for a sterile container, but found none. They were still on order. But I had several sterile aerosol sprayers. I put the unmodulated deplaquer in one of the aerosol spray bottles, which looked just like any off-the-shelf nasal spray container. I used a marker to carefully label the aerosol container "deplaquer without mod," and set it on my desk. It looked rather pitiful: a tiny white plastic container, the end result of a year of my life. *I'm not going to take a chance somebody takes this sample. I'll keep it with me for now.*

I dropped it in my purse and left the lab.

I walked through the glass doors into room 2030, the research director's office, at exactly 10 AM. I like being punctual.

Dr. DeSteele came out of her office to meet me. She was taller than I remembered (I'd had heels on at the party), but with the same commanding presence. She wore stylish indigo blue slacks and a bright yellow suit jacket, hair and makeup perfect, but not overdone. She was smiling a toothy smile. But this time I noticed how unhealthy she looked—her skin grayish and creased, her eyes red-rimmed. I guess at the party I'd been too excited to notice.

"Ms. Mechlin," she said, her voice as hoarse as a cigarette smoker's. "Thanks for coming on short notice." Her handshake was as short and sharp as I remembered.

She ushered me into her inner sanctum, which had a glass wall that overlooked the Coralville Campus's main entrance circle drive. The office was sumptuous but not palatial.

We sat down across from each other at the glass-topped table. She looked at me with her magnetic black eyes. Her assistant came in with two cups of coffee, cream, and sugar on a tray. She set them on the glass table and withdrew. DeSteele sipped from hers.

"Genetic engineering is the future of medicine," DeSteele said. "In the nineteenth century, medicine was about sanitation; in the twentieth century, chemicals and antibiotics—'bugs and drugs.'" Her predatory smile was almost scary. "But now we are moving beyond all those crude methods and dealing with infection and degeneration at the DNA level." She stared into my eyes, and I nodded dutifully. She was definitely charismatic. "And genetically engineered medical solutions are the future of this university. Yesterday's gene editing start-up firms like Sherlock, Mammoth, and Caribou have grown into multi-million dollar enterprises. Much of their basic research began at universities like this one. Start-up firms and established firms like Eli Lilly, Amgen, and Gilead provide millions of dollars of research money to institutions like UI, but they expect a return on their investment."

She leveled her smile at me, then raised her coffee cup to her lips. I reflexively sipped mine. "It's a special blend I particularly like," she said in an ingratiating tone.

I sipped mine. "It is very good."

"I'll come to the point, Ms. Mechlin. The Hathman Building is old and expensive to operate, and the university needs that building for other programs. Space is available for your research here at the Coralville facility, and you would have a significantly increased budget and priority access to the analytics staff. I'd like you to move your project here."

It was a great offer and there was no logical reason for me to refuse it. She knew it and I knew it. But the downside, and it was a big one, was that my research would now be behind an electronic security wall along with all the confidential corporate research. And walls work both ways. My findings would be safe from prying eyes, but I would also have to get clearance to share them with colleagues at other institutions, or to import their studies.

I sipped my coffee, stalling for time. All I could think of was the opera *Faust*, which I'd seen with my parents. The deal with the devil. The price seems trivial, but the final cost is horrendous.

"Our general fund has an unassigned line item in it," DeSteele continued. "I'd like to put your research project name on that line." Her eyes were steady on mine.

I put down my empty cup.

She leaned in and said as though imparting a confidence, "The security restrictions on projects here at the Coralville Campus are not trivial, I grant you. But the university would not be able to stay at the forefront of new technology without the constraints of confidentiality and patentability."

"I'd like to have a little time to think about this," I said.

She rose and walked me to her office door. "Yes, think about it, but I'd like to have your answer in twenty-four hours."

Back in my lab, I started up my computer, trying to think clearly, which seemed very difficult. *No surprise, after only a couple of hours of sleep last night.*

I ran a search of ongoing UI genetic engineering projects with inconclusive results, many projects related to genetics, but not gene editing. Then I ran a global search, but the result was a massive list of papers, most of them by Chinese researchers, titles and abstracts written in Mandarin. I tried a search for Susan's project and couldn't find it.

I went back to my examination of the outlier data set, then stopped. On a whim I got another swab sample from myself and put it and the sample from Leah's glass I'd heisted from the Airliner into the analyzer and set it in action.

While the analyzer worked, I studied my findings from last night at my apartment. Susan's modulator might actually reverse the effects of this mystery half edit I seemed to have identified. I ran the same analytic and got the same result as last night. It would reverse it.

The analyzer pinged, and I looked at the results on my computer. My sample fit the outlier data; Leah's did not. But Leah's sample did fit the general population curve perfectly. And my earliest sample fit the general population data too.

I thought I heard someone in the corridor, and today, instead of fear, I felt anger rising up inside me. I was sick and tired of all this. I got up, went to the door, and wrenched it open. The corridor was empty.

So what kind of bizarre experiment is the film school running? Someone gave many people, possibly everyone, a dose of a mood-altering gene edit. A gene edit that is badly designed. Half the time it will work with increasing effects, the other half of the time it won't work at all. That is ridiculous; nobody in their right mind would do that sort of thing. Absolutely immoral too—uncontrolled testing of some potentially mind- and body-altering substance without anyone's knowledge or permission.

I spent a futile ten minutes trying to view ongoing research at the Coralville Campus using my status as a fellow researcher, but I was denied access each time.

I felt very lonely with Susan gone. She would have made a good genetic engineer.

But she'll never be one. She'll be a housewife in a small town in Minnesota. But maybe she has the right idea. What's the point of doing great things in engineering if you come home to an empty apartment every night of your life?

I could walk away from all this, I thought. My parents would be shocked, but they would not scold me if I left UI behind and moved my research to another university. UCLA had a great program. Maybe Rick and I could move to LA together. But I knew that was completely unrealistic.

I thought I heard sounds in the corridor again, so I got up and went to the door and looked, but there was no one out there. I paced around the lab brushing my fingers over each of the familiar pieces of equipment. Susan's desk was neat—her chair pushed in, the desktop bare and dustless. But it always was. I envied Susan's neatness but could never quite seem to match it.

I guess maybe I understand why she quit. DeSteele's pressure to move was just the last straw. This life is too much work, and too lonely.

Suddenly I could no longer stand it in the cold lab. I grabbed my laptop and hurried up the stairs and out of the air lock into a hot summer afternoon.

I felt like I was emerging from a cave. The sunshine felt wonderful. I briskly walked the long block to the quadrangle. Under the big oak trees everything felt normal. But halfway around the quad my paranoia returned. I glanced back and tried to determine if any of the people on the sidewalks were following me.

Nobody seemed to be. I stopped at the sign that provides the history of the university and pretended to read it, letting people pass by. Still no one seemed to be following me. I glanced behind me one more time, and when I turned, I ran straight into a tall guy in a blue blazer.

"Sorry," I said, pulling back in fear.

"No harm done," he said. I stood frozen, half expecting him to grab me and carry me off. But instead he smiled affably. "Where are you going?"

"Arts and Science," I blurted, reluctant to mention the Hathman Building.

"Mind if I walk with you?" he said. "That's where I'm going too."

That was the last thing I wanted, but I smiled, thinking: *I can get away from this guy if he makes a move, so I'll just walk with him to Arts and Science then head back to my lab.*

"What field are you studying?"

"Anthropology," I improvised.

"Sounds interesting," the man said. "What kind of career does that lead to?"

"Usually puts you back in academia," I mumbled, making things up as I went.

"I spent some time in academia."

"You're on the faculty here?"

"I was. I'm retired now, but back here to take a writing course."

"You're a writer," I said, just talking to fill the time until I could get rid of him.

He laughed. "Learning to be one. I don't have anything significant in print yet."

"I hear it takes some time to learn to write."

"It's taking me a long time," he laughed. "But it's what I want to do. It's important to spend your life doing what you want to do. Too many people say they are miserable in their lives, but they don't make the effort to change their lives. I have little sympathy for them."

I nodded. "I used to love what I do…but lately there have been some problems…"

"Anything worth doing takes some effort. Maybe you need some help."

"Maybe, but there's no one I can ask for help."

"No one?" His eyebrows went up. "Surely there's someone you can trust. They can help you." He slowed. "Well I'm going in this door. You?"

"Yes. I mean no. I need to go by the Confucius Institute at that end of the building first," I fibbed.

"Well, so long," he said. "Good luck with your project. Find someone you trust and let them help you."

"Thanks," I said.

He paused, and was looking at me rather strangely. "Are you all right?"

"Yes, I'm fine. What name do I look for on the bestseller lists when you get your books published?"

He laughed. "Von Pittman," he said. Then he went up the steps and into the building.

I kept walking.

Back in my lab, I sat moping for a moment, staring at Susan's empty desk. I started thinking about where her desktop computer might be. I'd at first assumed the campus IT people took it for refurbishing. But I knew they never worked that fast. Campus IT usually took a week to respond to a service call. Whoever took it had access to this building. And I began to think they had no good reason to take it except under the assumption that the genetic modulator design was on the computer.

I quickly checked my purse to be sure I had the external drive Susan had given me. Whoever took her computer would not have her complete modulator design.

Paranoid again, I chastised myself. But I decided to leave the lab now. I eased the door open and moved quickly down the corridor, up the stairs, and through the airlock. I hurried away from the hedges around the building and got into my car.

I drove down Twelfth Street, started to turn on Maple toward my apartment, then changed my mind and crossed the river on the Iowa Avenue bridge and drove down Riverside Drive to Burlington. Then

I crossed back over the river, drove the length of campus, and made a series of random left and right turns on the residential streets near campus.

I drove past the parking garage at my apartment and continued on down Second Street, then abruptly turned into the parking garage at Leah's. I parked in visitor parking, texted her, and went up in the elevator.

Chapter Six

"You look terrible," Leah greeted me. "You want a glass of water? Some wine? A beer?"

"Some water."

When I'd choked some down, I sat on the sofa and poured out my fears. "The Hathman Building is double keyed. It takes one card to get in and out of the general access areas upstairs, and a second code on your key card to open the door to an individual lab. That second code also let Susan and me into the building after hours. But people are in there after hours, roaming around. I hear them. I think they're after me."

I set my glass on a coaster. I noticed my hands were shaking and folded them in my lap.

"Can they break into your lab? Like break the glass in the door?"

"The doors are all metal, but the old transoms above the doors are glass. Somebody might be able to break one and come through. They're about a foot tall and the width of the door."

Leah poured herself a glass of wine and lounged back in the easy chair near the windows. "I think you're probably just hearing things. You're tired. It's easy to get paranoid over nothing."

That was not the response I wanted.

"You don't believe me?" I asked peevishly. "There were people in the corridor of the Hathman Building last night, and I'm the only researcher left in that building…"

"I didn't know that."

"Yeah, there used to be eight of us in four labs on the lower level. Now there's only me. Most people left last semester. My labmate Susan just left the other day."

"I didn't know that either."

"I think she was pressured by Dr. DeSteele, the director of research."

"Pressured to do what?"

"Move to the Coralville Campus."

"What's wrong with that? I thought that facility was top-of-the-line, luxurious…"

"It is. But if you do your research there, it will fall under very strict information dissemination controls. You are giving up a lot of academic freedom, which is part of what research is about."

"You are sounding very paranoid again," Leah interrupted. "I've never heard of information controls on Arts and Science research."

"Because literature research is not weaponizable. I got an offer to move up to Coralville myself just this morning. And full funding for my project. Dr. DeSteele asked me to think it over."

Leah stared at me. "I'd say yes instantly if I were given that offer. Nobody in Arts and Sciences has full funding. And you should see the offices they give us. My cubicle is no bigger than that kitchen over there, and I share it with one other person. At the same time the university lets the so-called Confucius Institute take up half the first floor so they can throw fancy parties like the one where you and Rick...sorry, didn't mean to bring up painful issues."

To keep my mind off Rick, I asked, "What is the Confucius Institute anyway?"

Leah looked like her wine tasted bitter. "It's a Chinese-government sponsored 'cultural and language education center.' They are in universities all over the country. Recently I've been reading that some universities are kicking them out, saying they are spy and propaganda organizations. I wish we'd kick this one out, maybe then I'd get a proper office."

"It's funny you mention Chinese spying, because just the other day I was reading some info from the Genetic Engineering Community Committee about FBI arrests of researchers who had accepted money from Chinese organizations and illegally shared their research findings with the Chinese..." I stopped, exhausted. Too many negative things in my mind.

"I'd take that glass of wine now."

Leah brought me a glass of Chardonnay. The sharp cool taste of the wine reenergized me a bit.

"Let's forget about my paranoia for a moment. Here's what I think my sampling and data analysis says: somebody has administered a badly designed gene edit to a number of people on this campus without telling them..."

"What?" Leah sputtered. "That must violate every rule of professional ethics..."

"Let me finish, okay? The second thing I think I've found is that the gene edit that has been administered is flawed. It's only half an edit. And I can't for the life of me figure out why someone would use such a badly designed edit. Strangely, it closely resembles a gene edit developed to improve herd behavior in livestock. Actually, I should say, to correct anti-social behavior. I just stumbled on that fact when I was analyzing Susan's modulator, which this half edit resembles."

"Herd behavior?"

"Goats."

Leah laughed. "There are plenty of goatish people on this campus, so that part doesn't surprise me." A look crossed her face. "Who's been given this magic goat potion?"

"I don't know, but at least twenty-four people at the promo film party. You remember the glassware? All of them indicated the edit had been in the champagne."

"Including you?"

I nodded. "Yes. I ran another sample on myself, and I tested positive. And it's likely Rick got dosed also." I held out my empty glass and Leah filled it. "And here's a really puzzling fact—Susan's sample tested positive also. And I got that sample from her before the party."

"You got a sample from me before the party. Am I infected too?" Leah interrupted.

"It's not an infection. But in answer to your question, you show no evidence of the half edit. Not two weeks ago when you gave me a sample, and not yesterday when I took a second sample." I'd decided it was time for full disclosure. The advice I'd gotten from the stranger I'd bumped into on the quad was good—find somebody trustworthy and let them help. I trusted Leah.

"I took your glass from the Airliner, ran a sample check on it. You have not received this half edit."

Leah looked at me strangely. "I'm half-relieved and half-perturbed. Relieved I'm not 'edited' and perturbed you ran a sample on me without my permission. If you sample someone, you need to get their permission. Isn't that what all those signed forms are that I helped you collect when you set up your stand in the Arts and Science lobby a month ago?"

"Yes. I'm sorry I took that glass. I've not been myself lately."

"You seem to have become obsessed with glassware lately." She was trying to cheer me up.

"Well, I'm exhausted, paranoid, and confused. And really puzzled by why someone is doing this."

"Well, how about this," Leah said. "I'm familiar with magic elixirs. Half the ancient legends have one. They are usually used by the bad guys to induce the good guy to do something he doesn't want to. Like Siegfried deciding to marry Gutrune instead of Brünnhilde in the final volume of the…"

"No lectures tonight, Okay? I'm worn out."

"You asked for an explanation of why someone would do this," Leah said. "So hear me out. Someone wants people—the film school seniors at the party for example—to exhibit herd behavior, to follow instructions, to do what they're told."

I thought about it for a moment. "Could be, although this is a really crude way to…"

"But it's fast," Leah said. "History tells us that a new weapon, however imperfect, used in a timely manner wins battles, while a perfectly designed weapon that is too late doesn't win anything. You told me Rick's senior thesis film is due in a couple of days, right? And the promo films were two days ago. DeSteele wants these videos to say what she wants, right now, and she wants your project under her control right now."

"You are saying Dr. DeSteele is masterminding some scheme to get all UI research, current and future, and UI promotional videos focused on things she wants and directly under her control?"

"It could be," Leah said.

"Well she seems to want my project under her control. I'll admit that. She called me into her office today and gave me an offer I shouldn't refuse. And I drank a cup of coffee there. Probably got a second dose of that half edit."

"Jeez! What will a double dose do to you?" Leah was on her feet, her face knotted with concern.

"Nothing. If my genes have already been edited, then a second dose will have no effect. But I'll bet that's what happened to Susan. She met with DeSteele and drank coffee with this half edit in it. She fell into apathy—felt like it was too much trouble to move to Coralville, too much trouble to finish her doctorate—so she just quit and went home. Plus, even if my theory is right, which it could be, this method is really flawed. Ingestion is a very imperfect way of administering a gene edit, and because it is improperly designed, it will only affect about 50 percent of the people it's given to. The rest will have no hormonal change. So maybe Rick and I are in the lucky 50 percent; I don't know. I'm not an endocrinologist, but I expect the symptoms would first be apathy, a tendency to do what someone tells you to do. Later, as the gene expression becomes more pronounced, feelings of paranoia, depression…I don't know where it might end. I feel depressed and apathetic, and paranoid. This is not the real me. I know it's not, but I can't help myself."

"Can this toxin be eliminated once you have it?" Leah asked in a very subdued tone.

I shook my head. "No. Well, in this case, maybe. A properly done gene edit cannot be reversed, but this one is only half done, so the body might re-edit the faulty DNA strand as part of its normal maintenance…"

Leah poured herself some more wine and held the bottle up toward me. I shook my head no. "I'd suggest we call Campus Security, but if DeSteele is behind it, they won't be any help."

I was thinking. Gene edits can be reversed by administering a second edit that eliminates the first edit. But for me to synthesize a re-edit and properly administer it to myself and Rick and a bunch of other people while DeSteele was fighting me every step of the way seemed overwhelming. Better to just wait and see if my body and Rick's would reject the half edit and stop the hormonal changes. I just wanted all this to end.

"Hey," Leah said. "You're going to fall asleep and spill that wine on my sofa." She got some sheets, a blanket, and a pillow from her bedroom. "You're spending the night here tonight. Help me fold out this sofa bed."

I nodded. "Why would these conspirators administer a gene edit by ingestion? That is the worst method. The only way to get the dosage right is intravenously. A remote second-best would be an inhaler, moving the enzyme straight through mucus membranes...but ingestion? Stomach acids would destabilize..."

"Stop talking," Leah said. "You need rest." I got into the sofa bed. Before turning off the living room light, Leah said, "I do take what you say seriously, and I'll help do whatever is needed to get you and Rick cured. I told you a possible scenario, but frankly, it sounds really...strange. See if you think it sounds as looney as I think it does. You've uncovered a conspiracy by Dr. DeSteele to increase herd behavior in the film school by feeding them a magic potion based on goat research. The genetic alteration is apparently being conducted by idiots, since the magic potion doesn't work right and they are using the wrong method to administer it. The objective is for DeSteele to control all UI research. And, oh yes, unknown persons are creeping around your lab building, probably coming after you. Jeez, what a story."

I fell into an exhausted sleep.

The next morning, Leah brewed some of that great coffee she makes and set out two containers of the yogurt she loves, but I hate. It's the stuff with the fruit on the bottom. It's more like eating a strawberry sundae than anything healthy. But I put a smile on my face and sat down with her at the little round kitchen table and drank my coffee. The coffee was good.

After the caffeine started working, Leah began, "Looks like you are feeling better this morning. Last night you were a little, what shall I say? Overwrought?"

I thought about it. *Maybe my analyses are wrong. My fear may only be in my own mind. Maybe there's some perfectly rational explanation. I probably don't feel well because I'm tired and stressed about Rick and me, and about DeSteele's "offer."*

"Maybe I am over-reacting," I told Leah.

"Will you look into how this theoretical half edit works and how to reverse it?"

"Yeah," I said.

I peeled the foil off the yogurt and began folding the foil into ever smaller squares. Leah watched this with a raised eyebrow. "I know you've got a lot on your mind," she said, "but don't forget you are a student with an in-progress report to your thesis committee due in a few days, if I remember what you told me."

"Yeah," I repeated.

"Forget my DeSteele-conquers-the-world hypothesis for a minute. Aside from your fatigue and possible suspicious noises in the hall of your lab, which could have been entirely innocent, all that's really happened is that Rick asked for some time to focus on his senior thesis film, Susan left school, and you got a wonderful offer to do your work in the Coralville labs."

"Yeah," I said again.

She held the coffee pot up, but I shook my head no.

"Stay here today," Leah offered. "You've got your laptop with you, as always. Work on your project here."

I sat there staring at my coffee cup. "Thanks. I do need some place away from my lab. Some place I can think all this through AND do some analysis work on my project."

Leah stood up and tossed her yogurt container in the trash. "Well, I've got to get to class since I'm TA for European history this semester and class is all the way over in McAlester Hall. You stay here as long as you want." She gave me a hug and left.

I sat there at the microscopic kitchen table, staring at the lush lawns of the apartment complex courtyard.

Finally I dumped the rest of my yogurt down the garbage disposal, rinsed out my coffee cup, and opened my laptop. But I couldn't seem to focus. I paced around the apartment for a while trying to decide if I should stay here and work or go someplace else. I needed about six hours to get Susan's enzyme tailored to my gene clipper. Then I'd run some analytics to make sure the combination worked right.

I might want to go ahead and synthesize some of the modulator and keep it with me. That way I'd have my laptop with all my data, and samples of both parts of my deplaquer in case I have to leave UI, or even if I just move to the Coralville Campus.

I opened my laptop and slogged away for almost an hour before my mind bogged down. I felt really fatigued, even though I'd slept fairly well last night.

I saved my analytics to the correct files, then lay down on the couch. I was tired but not sleepy. I wished everything was back the way it had been a week ago. No—the way it had been two months ago, early spring, when I first met Rick.

Leah and I were at this little film festival on campus. Rick had a film in it, a five-minute documentary that was actually a lot better than I was expecting. After the films, there was a "meet the filmmaker" reception, which wasn't too crowded. While we were sipping our wine, I told Leah, "That guy looks like Steve McQueen." She grabbed my elbow and we went up to him and told him we'd enjoyed his film. We all introduced ourselves, and things developed from there. Leah and I both thought he was really good looking and cool. Leah liked him, but had the courtesy to step aside when I told her I REALLY liked him and he'd already asked me out.

From the beginning, Rick and I got along great. We went to Hamburg Inn #2 (there's a long story behind that name, and yes, years ago there was a Hamburg Inn #1), had something to eat, and told each other a few bits and pieces about our pasts. Turned out he was from Chicago too. Berwyn. Not far from my parents' house in Lakeshore.

We talked for more than an hour. It started raining—a warm spring rain—so he ordered a couple of peach lemonades (which were hideous, but I drank as much as I could of mine with a smile on my face since he'd ordered them). Then he talked about films. He was in the process of making the film for his senior thesis. "I need to pick your brain," he told me with that smile I already loved. "See, my film is about the spread of infection in urban settings. Not just disease, but psychological infections like hopelessness, dependency—meaning generation after generation on welfare, that kind of thing. And since you're in biomedicine..."

"I'm not an epidemiologist, but I'll be happy to tell you what I know. You've got to remember that I'm just a doctoral candidate with a really narrow field of specialization." I described my project to him and he seemed interested. "The potential for genetic engineering to reduce human misery is enormous," I told him. But I didn't want to bore him so let the conversation shift back to films. And somewhere in the midst of it he asked me out on a second date, to go see a movie at the ArtHouse Theater.

"They're showing Antonioni's *Blow-up*." He paused for my reaction.

I had never heard of Antonioni, but I'd heard something about a film named *Blow-up*, I think.

Rick pretended to be shocked. "I can see by your expression how widespread cinematic illiteracy is in this country." He laughed. "*Blow-up* is THE quintessential 1960s film. That's way before our time, I know, but it was an important decade for many reasons. And in *Blow-up*, Antonioni caught the atmosphere and attitudes of 1966 'Swinging London' perfectly. He also made some wonderful statements about reality and illusion and about losing the meaning of something if you examine it too closely. Also there's...sorry...I tend to ramble on when talking about films. It starts at seven. I could pick you up, but there's no parking anywhere near the theater, and I think it would be easier just to walk there."

"I'd love to go. I'll meet you at the theater a little before seven," I told him.

We saw each other every few days after that. And our relationship developed quickly, but not too quickly. Rick's got a great body, and he seemed to like mine, but believe it or not, we didn't spend all our time having sex. He is passionate about his filmmaking, and I really care about my research, so our time together was limited.

I was sorry now we hadn't spent more time together.

Chapter Seven

I forced myself to my feet, collected my laptop, and walked out of Leah's apartment complex. I decided to leave my car in her apartment's visitor parking space in case somebody knew my car and was following it. *I'll walk to campus, but first a stop for more coffee.*

The four-block walk to River Styx coffee shop got my blood flowing again. There's something about being outside, the oak trees overhead, birds cheerful, that makes you realize the universe is a big place and our little concerns are just that—little concerns.

I got a latte and took a seat at a table near the front windows so I could see who was coming in, but they wouldn't immediately see me.

I opened my files and resumed work. I had to segment the operations on the laptop due to processing power, but I could still get it done. In the lab, my desktop computer could do it all simultaneously. But at least this way, the slow way, I could check each step as I went along. The ambiance of the coffee shop helped me keep my energy up. Leah's apartment had just been too silent. And the lab was too spooky.

But while I waited for the laptop to work through a long sequence of calculations, I found myself covertly checking the people around me. There was an older guy reading a book, two middle-aged women, three loud guys jabbering away. Nobody suspicious. But what would a suspicious person look like?

I turned my attention back to my computer.

Since I had to synthesize each of the two parts separately, I decided to finish the design and list the steps to synthesize Susan's modulator first.

I took the enzyme composition and worked backward to get the components, then ran an analysis to see what available compounds could be used to make them and what process would be needed to get them combined into the proper end-compound. I was once again absorbed in my work, my paranoia displaced by the pure enjoyment of interesting challenges.

My laptop only has limited simulation capabilities, but I used what I had to do a simulation of the effects of Susan's modulator not connected to my deplaquer. And I ran a simulation of the half edit I reverse-engineered from the information in the glassware samples. The similarities were striking. And more than that, the modulator could be used to eliminate the half edit. But I would have to run full-scale simulations on my desktop computer in my lab to be sure.

When I glanced at the clock on the wall it was nearly noon.

I stared around the coffee shop, which had mostly cleared out as people left for lunch. One old guy left, sitting by the window staring out at the passersby. Wispy gray-white hair, soft body, pasty skin, short pants. *Probably a retired professor whose wife doesn't want him hanging around the house all day, and he's got nowhere else to go. Hasn't done any original work since his doctorate. Spent his career teaching meaningless courses to kids who didn't want to be in his class. I don't want to end up like that.*

I closed my laptop and sat staring at my empty cup. It seemed like too much effort to do anything but sit here.

I could quit now, go with Rick to LA, find a job in genetic engineering...no, without a PhD I'd never get a job I really wanted. I'd never be allowed to work on cutting-edge genetic engineering, never really make a contribution toward the health care of the future.

I left money on the table and went out into an Iowa summer day already hot enough to keep people walking in the shade of the store awnings.

A block from the coffee shop I stopped and pretended to look at a bookstore display window, but in reality I was trying to determine if anyone was following me.

"Better get in out of the sun, young lady," an old woman in a straw sunhat told me as she passed. I stepped under the awning of the gift shop next door to the bookstore. I continued to stand there, not wanting to go to my lab, but knowing I needed to. Finally I sighed, squared my shoulders, and walked to Leah's apartment parking garage to get my car.

At the Hathman Building there were no cars in the parking lot. I hurried inside and down to my lab. *This is crazy,* I thought, *there are no intruders. There's nobody after me.* But I couldn't concentrate. Telling myself I was just taking a break, I went to the lab door and listened. There was no sound in the corridor. But what if someone with a passkey does come after me? There was an emergency exit on each floor at the end of the corridor. The door would be alarmed of course, and would signal Campus Security. But I could get out and get away from somebody chasing me. I didn't remember exactly what the end of the building looked like, but I thought I remembered there were concrete steps up from the emergency exit to ground level.

But if someone could get in the front door, I wouldn't have much of a chance. Unless the front door was locked so that even a passkey couldn't open it. And there was a way to do that. I rummaged in my desk until I found an old-fashioned ruler, then went upstairs to the front airlock door.

I waved my passkey over the door lock and the inner glass doors slid open. Then I stepped back into the building and let the inner doors slide closed against my ruler set edgewise, holding the door open a couple of millimeters. I pulled the ruler in slightly so it might not be noticed right away by someone outside trying to get in.

Some air whistled through the space, but not such a big draft it would overload the air system and trigger an alarm. I hoped.

Since the inner door was not closed, the outer door would not open even to someone with a passkey.

Feeling much safer, I went back to my lab and sat down at my computer. I put in the 3D images of Susan's modulator and my reverse-engineered copy of the half edit and ran full-scale simulations of their effects and how or if they might counter each other.

I was expecting this to take several minutes and that I would be provided with a long list of partial solutions. But in less than a minute the computer showed me only one solution. And it had a probability of 98 percent accuracy. Susan's modulator would reverse the half edit and do it very quickly and efficiently.

But when I thought about it for a moment, I realized it shouldn't be surprising. Both Susan's modulator and this half edit fit the same location on the DNA helix. The modulator snips out a section of DNA so that it can be replaced by my deplaquer. But if there is no deplaquer, the modulator will simply snip out the half edit, blood phages will destroy it, and the DNA strand will heal itself by copying itself since nothing new has been inserted.

I've found a way to undo the half edit. I can synthesize some of Susan's modulator, but I only have 9 cc of enzyme left, so I can only make a few dosages. But I had no way of testing them. I glanced at the clock and realized I needed to contact DeSteele's office. She'd asked for my decision about moving to Coralville within twenty-four hours, and it had been more than that.

But I'm going to decline her offer. I don't think she's going to take drastic action against me in the next day or two. I hope.

Dreading the conversation to come, I picked up my phone and called the Research Directorate front office. "I'd like to speak to Dr. DeSteele. This is Francesca Mechlin. She asked me to call her."

"I'm afraid she is gone for the day. Would you like her voicemail?"

I tried to make my statement on her voicemail as polite as possible, thanking her for the offer, but explaining that I wanted to complete this phase of my work here at the Hathman Building. I left the issue of my moving to Coralville in the future open.

I put DeSteele out of my mind, got out my remaining 9 cc of enzyme, and measured out 3 cc each into two glass pipettes that I put in the airbox along with reagents and tools. In a few moments I had synthesized two doses of Susan's modulator—one for me, one for Rick. That left me just enough enzyme to make one more modulator, which I would combine with the deplaquer to have a full prototype for my project.

I put each dose of modulator I'd made in a separate aerosol nasal spray bottle and marked them "modulator." I was on the point of dropping them in my purse, when on impulse I put one bottle to my nose and shot a good sniff up each of my nostrils.

"To hell with a testing regime, this stuff either works or it doesn't."

I stood there a moment, appalled at what I had just done.

Chapter Eight

I put the dose I intended for Rick in my purse. Gene edits work fast, but I felt no different than I had this morning.

I rechecked my analytics on the modulator, and everything checked out. It was correctly formulated and should work to immediately clip out the half-edited gene sequence.

I carefully rechecked my entire sequence again to be absolutely sure it would clip out the half edit *and only the half edit.*

I heard sounds in the corridor again. I froze, but I heard nothing more. After a minute I went back to work and thought I heard them again. Again I stopped and listened, but there was nothing.

It was 5 PM. I knew Leah should be out of her last class by now, so I texted her. *Can I come over to your place?*

She texted right back: *Sure.*

She handed me a glass of Chardonnay as soon as I walked in the door.

"Well, you look more cheerful," she told me. She sat down in her easy chair and I sat on the sofa. I took a long drink of my wine, took a deep breath, and told about finding a "reverser" for the mystery half edit.

"Wait a minute!" Leah exploded. "Don't tell me you tried this concoction on yourself!"

"I did."

"Trying out untested drugs! Don't you know how dangerous that is?" Leah sputtered.

"It's not a drug."

"Not to mention being completely outside any reasonable professional rules of conduct."

"I know. But last night I told you how I'd been feeling the last couple of days, depressed and all. Well, I took a dose of it two hours ago and I am beginning to feel much better. I need to get some to Rick."

"And I suppose you're going to dose him without his knowledge, right?"

"I'm afraid he won't take it otherwise." I paused. "I was hoping you might be able to get him to take some, in a drink of water maybe; it's completely tasteless…"

"Jeez!" I heard Leah take a deep breath. "Well, I'm your friend, so I'll help you if I can, but I sure hope you know what you're doing. I still think explaining things to him would be best. He's smart…"

"But DeSteele's toxin as you call it works on your emotions, clouding your judgment. I don't think he's going to want to listen and believe this…and besides, we need to work fast. This is an emergency, so the end justifies the means."

"That's what Heinrich Himmler said."

There was a long silence.

"I can't think of any way I can get him to drink something," Leah said. "If he won't see you, he won't see me…"

"He's really busy right now. His thesis film is due… and he's having difficulties with it. People are giving him last-minute instructions…"

"People like the Confucius Institute people?"

"I don't know. Maybe."

"I know there is a mandatory meeting of film school seniors tomorrow morning, in the CI. It was on the UI network notices for our building. Those people have half the building…"

"What time is the meeting tomorrow?"

"Eight."

"I don't want to see DeSteele, so I'm not going to go inside in case she's in the meeting, but maybe I can catch Rick just before he goes into the building. Hand him a drink, a cup of coffee, with the reverser in it."

She nodded thoughtfully.

"Mind if I spend the night here?" I asked. My paranoia had subsided considerably, but why take a chance?

"I insist you stay here tonight," Leah said.

The next morning was breezy and mild, and I felt better than I had for days—clear-headed and energized. I was standing on the steps of the Arts and Science Building with two paper cups of coffee from Campus Shoppes. One of them contained a dose of my reverser, which I hoped to induce Rick to drink. I hated not telling him what I was doing, but I thought it better to get the stuff into him, then once his head cleared, like mine had, tell him what I'd done. He's a great guy; I knew he would forgive me. But still…my heart was pounding.

I spotted him coming down the shady sidewalk from the student parking lot. I felt a rush of longing. *Focus on the moment,* I told myself.

I put a smile on my face. "Hi Rick."

Close up he looked awful—fatigue lines in his face and a shadowed look in his eyes. I had no doubt DeSteele's poison was the cause. He accepted the cup I handed him without a word. "I've only got a minute," he said.

"Rick, I know you are under a lot of pressure, and I know we decided not to see each other for a while," I looked down at my coffee. "But I just wanted you to know that I'm behind you all the way. I want your project to succeed, I want you to succeed, and if there's anything I can do to help…"

I took a drink of my coffee hoping he would follow suit. "Some caffeine might help," I nudged.

He stared at the cup. "Maybe." He looked at me with an expression I'd never seen on his face before: hopelessness. Usually he was calm, quiet, and confident—but not now.

He shrugged. "I've got one more day to get my film edited and submitted. And now I'm getting all kinds of instructions from these people," he tilted his head toward the building, "telling me to be sure the film emphasizes this, be sure there are some hints of that, all this crap…" He stared at the coffee. "It's impossible to make those kinds of changes at this stage of the project. It all seems so difficult. I'm just a machine these days doing what these people tell me to. I'll submit my film, but it's not going to be any good. I need a break…"

My heart took a sudden leap. *Maybe Rick would stay in Iowa City a few more days!*

I put my hand on his arm. "I know you can do it. Your film will be good. You're just having last minute doubts."

He shook his head, not meeting my eye. "I need to get inside to this meeting. It's mandatory." He took a small drink of his coffee. "I'll talk to you soon. And, thanks Fran, for your support."

He turned and went in through the glass doors. I saw him toss his coffee cup in the trash.

I could only hope that he had drunk enough for the reverser to work.

Chapter Nine

I realized a couple of Chinese men who were standing beside the door to the auditorium weren't watching the students filing in, they were watching me. They saw me looking at them and hurried off down the hallway. Suddenly fearful, I turned and ran down the sidewalk to the quad, then slowed my pace and attempted to blend in with students walking to their classes. Then I walked to Leah's apartment building where I'd left my car. Inside the echoing parking garage, I stood a moment in the shadows to see if anyone had followed me, but no one had.

I got in my car then felt in my purse. The two aerosol sprayers were still there. I pulled out the one labeled "modulator" and shook it. It was empty. The other one, labeled "deplaquer without mod," still had the full 3 cc charge in it.

I need to get to my lab, synthesize more modulator, and combine some of it with deplaquer. Then I will have samples of both components and a sample of the final product with me. I could leave Iowa City and go to another university... No, that would take a lot of time and effort. I need to complete my degree here. And try to help people who have been treated with this half edit. But to do that I have to get DeSteele off my back.

But if someone is following me, they will likely know this car. And since it is the only one in the parking lot when I'm in my lab, they'll know I'm there.

I thought about this for a moment, then texted Leah: *If you are at home, can I come by?*

I'll be home in about ten minutes.

See you then.

I sat in my car waiting for ten minutes to pass. I kept craning around trying to see if anyone was in the parking garage, creeping up on me in the car. But there was no movement. I know people can be tracked by their cell phones, but I'd read that takes a lot of software, and I didn't think DeSteele and her Chinese accomplices had taken that step. Not yet anyway.

I got out of my car and took the elevator up to Leah's apartment.

"Come in, come in," Leah said, always cheerful. "Did you get Rick to take the elixir?"

"Yeah. I met him at your building just now, gave

him some coffee with the mix in it. He sipped some, hopefully enough to get into his blood through his stomach, which is not easy. I'll text him tomorrow and see if he notices anything."

In the living room I discarded my purse and sprawled on the sofa.

"You should spend tonight here again," Leah said. "Even though you say you feel better, you have still been working too hard. On the other hand, you are making progress. You know DeSteele and her minions are dosing people with this evil potion, and you've devised an elixir to counter it, right? Problem solved."

"The problem is not solved," I said. "DeSteele and her Chinese handlers are still after me; I should say after my deplaquer design." I tapped my purse. "I'm scared to go to my lab, but I need to synthesize more modulator so I've got something to demonstrate that there is a half edit being given to people and that my modulator will reverse it. But I have no idea who the right people are to explain all this to."

Leah looked thoughtful. "I don't know who the right people are either. The director of research is equal to a dean and sits on the executive committee, I think. So there's nobody above them except the president of the university. I think it's unlikely the president would listen to your story, much less do anything about it."

I nodded. "I agree. And I think persons unknown, but likely working for DeSteele or the Chinese..." I sat up straight. "You know, DeSteele may be working for the Chinese, not the other way around."

"Could be," Leah said. "In which case we've really got to be careful. There's more at stake here than just DeSteele's desire to control research. Who knows what the Chinese might do to get what they want."

We fell silent for a moment. "But, in the meantime, I've got enough ingredients in my lab to make one more dose of modulator. And with that as a sample, we've got something to show someone who might be able to resolve all this. But I hate to go to my lab alone. I'd feel a lot safer if you came with me."

She was silent for another moment.

"It won't take me long to synthesize more modulator... maybe thirty minutes at most."

Leah considered this. "Right now?"

"Yes."

"Okay."

"Can we take your car?"

Leah sighed. "Okay."

"And let's don't park in the Hathman parking lot but on Eleventh Street. Then we walk across the back lawn and around the building to the front door. We slip inside, I'll get my work done as quickly as possible, and we get out."

Leah nodded slowly. "Okay, let's go."

Leah parked on Eleventh Street. We had driven by the building on Twelfth Street to see if there were cars in the parking lot. There were none. We walked quickly across the lawn and I cycled us through the airlock with my passkey. Inside, I stopped long enough to insert my ruler to keep the inner door slightly open. "Keeps the outer door locked," I explained.

We hurried downstairs to my lab and I set to work.

Leah sat on the lab stool and watched as I measured out the last of my enzyme and put it in the airbox with my other tools.

Synthesizing is delicate work, and you need to be precise, but it is not difficult work.

It wasn't long before I took the glass pipette out of the airbox and transferred the fluid to another clean aerosol container.

"That little bit of transparent liquid is all there is to it?" Leah asked.

"That's it. It's entirely odorless, tasteless, colorless. The only way to determine it is there is by a very specialized chemical analysis. But this minute bit of fluid carries many, many little gene splicers. Little robots that quickly rebuild the human body."

"Do you know how dangerous all this sounds? And how risky?" Leah whispered. "That stuff could be anywhere and people would not know."

I nodded. "True, but let's don't hang around here talking; let's get going." I cleaned up my apparatus and dropped the aerosol into my purse.

"You haven't done proper testing on any of this have you?" Leah said.

"No, I…"

There was a very faint noise from outside the lab door. It could have been upstairs at the front door. Leah and I froze.

"Let's get out of here right now," Leah whispered.

I stepped to the door and swiped my passkey past the card reader. The light stayed red. I tried it again, but the light remained a steady red. I tried pulling the door, but it was still firmly locked.

"They deactivated your key!" Leah said. "Now what?"

I pointed at the transom. "We break out the glass, slide through, and run for the exit door at the end of the corridor."

Leah hoisted a metal lab stool.

I pulled out my phone. "I'll call Rick. We need a getaway car waiting for us when we break out. I don't think we can get past them to your car."

There was more noise from outside the lab, louder this time. And it was definitely coming from the front door upstairs.

"I'll break the glass while you call Rick," Leah said. "Hurry."

I called him and he answered immediately, thank God. "Leah and I are in the Hathman Building and people are after us. We're going out the fire exit at the end of the building. Can you pick us up on Maple Street?"

"Your timing is good. I'm in my car driving home, so I can be there in five minutes."

Leah took one practice swing, then hurled the lab stool up and at the glass transom. Broken glass blew out into the corridor and the lab stool fell back at our feet. We could hear a racket from the airlock at the front of the building. People were definitely trying to break in. Leah set up the lab stool so we could stand on it and get through the transom. "Not even bent," Leah noted. "Good quality; American made."

I grabbed two lab smocks, stood on the lab stool, and laid them on the frame and bits of broken glass. With my purse in one hand, I slid through and dropped to the floor. Leah was beside me in a minute.

I grabbed her hand and pulled her along. "Come on!"

There was a tremendous crash from upstairs. "Sounds like they're in the building," Leah said.

Hoping the automated systems couldn't lock fire doors, I jammed down hard on the panic bar and pushed. The steel door creaked open and the fire alarm started blaring.

We scrambled up concrete stairs littered with dirt and leaves, then bolted across the lawn and into the line of trees along Maple Street. Rick's black Dodge was just pulling to the curb. Leah and I tumbled into the car, and Rick smoked the tires getting us out of there.

"Anybody following us?" he asked Leah in the back seat.

"Can't see anybody," Leah said. "I think we made it."

Rick turned to me. "We're going to my apartment. Nobody knows where I live, do they?"

"I doubt it," I said. My heart was pounding.

"Then I want to know what the hell is going on," Rick said.

Chapter Ten

Rick took the long way around to his apartment—Melrose and then Hawkins Drive, then back on Highway 6, not speeding, just keeping up with traffic.

"How do you feel, Rick?" I asked once my heart rate slowed.

"About this little escapade?"

"No, in general."

"Well, actually I feel better now than I have for several days."

I turned to Leah in the back seat and we nodded to each other.

Rick's frown was deep. "I suspect you weren't just asking to be polite."

I took a deep breath and said, "I gave you a gene edit in your coffee this morning when we met in front of Arts and Science. What I gave you was intended to reverse a dose of a different gene edit you got at the promo film party. It seems like it is working. I'm sorry.

I should have explained everything to you, but there was no time, and—I'm sorry."

Leah leaned on the back of the front seat. "Fran has convinced me that Dr. DeSteele is doing some really outrageous stuff. Today, after dodging those guys back there, I'm convinced she's right. There's some kind of conspiracy right here on campus, and DeSteele is in the middle of it."

Rick said nothing as we made our way back to his apartment building. In the parking garage, he shut off the engine and we all sat there in silence for a moment more. "Let's wait a minute," Rick said. "Be sure nobody has followed us." His eyes were on the rearview mirror.

"I got some of the same stuff," I told him, "and my emotions have been on a roller coaster since then. But I took some of the gene edit I gave you, and I feel better. I'm glad you do too."

Rick nodded. "What you're saying is hard to believe, but if it's true, it would explain a lot. Let's go inside."

The parking garage was silent as the three of us moved quickly to the elevator and up to Rick's apartment. Inside, he assured himself the door was locked, then sat down beside me on the sofa. Leah slumped into the easy chair by the window. I was shaking; the adrenaline of the chase was dissipating.

But at the same time I also felt much better. Rick's familiar apartment, the two people I trusted most in the world here with me. I wouldn't have to try to resolve all these problems by myself.

Rick took my hand and I felt my heart glow. "Are you okay?" he asked, and I nodded.

After a while, we drank some cold water. Rick's place is always clean and neat. I made the same mental note I always made when I visited his place—keep my place cleaner and neater.

"So what is DeSteele doing and what's it got to do with these drugs we're all getting and what's it got to do with guys chasing you out of your lab?"

I could not quite suppress a shudder. "That's a lot of questions I can't answer," I said. "I think somebody, I believe it is Dr. DeSteele, wants my research project. They want me to move to the Coralville Campus where I'll be under their control. I don't want to do that, and they are getting more aggressive. They took my desktop computer, but I didn't leave a full file set there. I think they administered a dose of a gene edit to people at your promo film party to try to get all of you more docile, more susceptible to following instructions, to making your films her way."

Rick started to say something, paused, then said, "Who's 'they'? But before you answer that, let me tell you this: I think back to how I've been thinking and acting in the last couple of days, and it's like I was somebody else. And me and all the other seniors have been getting all sorts of directions from DeSteele's office about how to shoot our films. But my mood was such that it was simpler to just go along with what they were telling me...even though I was really messing up my film. I hated it, but I went along with it."

Leah set her water glass aside. "So you both, and others, were drugged into DeSteele's zombie army, receiving instructions from the fortress of ultimate darkness. Sorry, I'm joking at a bad time, but I'm a lit major—I can't help making a story out of life...but back to the problem at hand. What do we do now? But before either of you answers that, think about this: the UI research director, Dr. DeSteele, wants an integrated set of promotional films showing all the kinds of cutting-edge research the university is doing, all the great facilities, with the intent of using them to attract world-class researchers here to UI. It all seems logical. Maybe there is no conspiracy."

"Maybe," I said. "But there is a very strange half edit being dispensed to people without their consent. I don't like it. A bunch of people have been treated with a half-baked gene edit, without telling them, which is grossly unprofessional."

She gave me a look. "I won't mention you taking an untested reverser and later giving some to Rick without telling him."

"Never mind that now," Rick said. "Maybe it's just my scriptwriting sense, making stories, but what if DeSteele herself is under someone else's influence. All this UI propaganda and the consolidation of genetic engineering projects behind security screens..."

"That's what I'm thinking," Leah said. "DeSteele spends a lot of time at that Chinese-front Confucius Institute in Arts and Science. Sounds like a Chinese Communist plot and DeSteele is one of their puppets. Far-fetched but not impossible."

"That's not so far-fetched," Rick told her. "The Chinese government is attempting to dominate the world's economy, and they are doing all sorts of things to make that happen, like infiltrating the 5G communications systems being deployed worldwide. My soundman was one of the meeting attendees in the Confucius Institute, and he went wandering around in the back rooms. He said there's some really sophisticated electronics in there, and everyone was Chinese, speaking only Chinese. I wouldn't be surprised if they have secure communications back to China."

We sat there looking at each other.

Rick heaved a sigh. "Well if this is true, we've got a problem too big for us to handle."

"We can't get rid of the Confucius Institute," I said, "not immediately, although other universities have. And just going to University Administration or the police won't work. It's just our word against theirs, and I'm sure they would have a convincing cover story. But maybe we can somehow deflect DeSteele from the course she's on."

"That's one nice thing about totalitarian organizations," Leah said. "Get rid of the top dog, and the system falls apart."

"Assuming DeSteele is the top dog," Rick said.

"I said *deflect* DeSteele," I told them. "I don't want to harm her, not physically—that's wrong. I can't do that."

"Me neither," Leah agreed. "So what other options do we have to get DeSteele out of the picture? Can you hype-up this 'mood enhancer' she's using on people, turn it against her?"

I shook my head. "No. It's not like a drug where you can change the dosage and get a different effect. A gene edit is a single-acting treatment...so all we can do is give her some of my modulator, which will negate the half edit, assuming she's been dosed too, which is not a certainty."

"We dose DeSteele with your modulator and she suddenly becomes a kinder, gentler person, and quits working for the Chinese?" Leah said with a laugh.

"Don't laugh," I told her. "This stuff works fast. And moods influence our thinking on quite a deep level. It might work. And besides, it's the only thing I can think of we can do immediately. So where shall we intercept her?"

"She comes to A&S at least a couple of times a week," Leah said. "In the afternoon, about the same time I'm getting out of my Seventeenth Century Lit and Music class," she glanced at the clock, "which I missed today because I had to participate in your little escape from the Hathman catacombs."

Rick got up to pace, then stopped and peered out the edge of the closed drapes. He turned to me. "There's no downside to using it on her, right?"

"Right," I said. "If she does not have the half edit, the reverser will have no effect on her, but if she does, she should start changing within a couple of hours."

"And by the way," Rick said, smiling at me. "Thanks. I'm glad you got some of that stuff into me."

I took his hand. "That half edit we got dosed with is dangerous. It scares me to think that somebody is willing to administer this stuff widely just to manipulate people. They don't know or care about the long-term effects."

"Poor Susan," Leah said softly.

"What happened to her?" Rick asked.

"I think DeSteele gave Susan a dose of this stuff last week," I said. "Then pressured her to move to the secure labs at Coralville…"

"Just like they are pressuring you, right?"

"Right. And Susan couldn't deal with it, so she simply left the university." I touched my purse with Susan's external computer drive in it. "Fortunately she gave me her modulator design before she left."

"Poor thing," Leah repeated. "She was a really nice person, very quiet. Not like me."

Rick glanced at the clock in the kitchen. "Anyway… do we have any other options? If DeSteele is going to the CI this afternoon we can try to intercept her there if we get there in the next thirty minutes."

"What about talking to Campus Security?" Leah suggested. "Or the Iowa City police?"

"DeSteele can control the campus cops," Rick said. "And trying to explain theft of research secrets and a genetic edit to the city police seems like a futile effort."

"Well," Leah said. "Let's try your drug on DeSteele. It sounds like it's our only option."

"It's not a drug," I told her for the hundredth time.

Chapter Eleven

We filed out of Rick's apartment into his car and idled down Second Avenue in light traffic. The afternoon light was turning gold. I was so tense I could barely contain myself. *To just be able to enjoy an Iowa summer afternoon with nothing more on my mind than completing my research, that's all I want. I don't need all this stuff—threats and suspicions, DeSteele and Chinese spying.*

Rick looked my way and took my hand. "It's going to be all right. We'll get through this."

I nodded.

"You sure you don't want me to do the dirty work?" he asked.

"No," I said. "She'll remember me from our meeting, so there's a good chance I can attract her attention, get her to stop and talk to me. If I move fast, she won't have time to get defensive."

"I don't like you being so close to her," Rick said.

"Leah will be behind me ready to help out if necessary. DeSteele does not know Leah, so she should be able to remain unnoticed." I was trying to sound confident, but I was quaking with fear. *What if DeSteele's assistant confronts me? What if the Chinese guys in the building come after me?*

I'd just have to move fast and hope for the best.

Rick pulled to a stop at the end of the Arts and Science Building. Leah and I got out, and I started down the sidewalk heading for the entrance. Leah stayed at a discreet distance behind me. The sidewalk was crowded with students.

Ahead, I saw someone starting up the steps through the crowd of students coming out of the building.

It was DeSteele and she was early!

I pushed my way through the people on the sidewalk. A couple of Chinese men were in the lobby. One was holding one of the glass doors open for her. I struggled up the stairs, one hand in my purse. "Dr. DeSteele!" I shouted. She turned.

"Ah, it's you, Ms. Mechlin," DeSteele said. "I got your message declining my offer, but that is unacceptable. I want you to move your research to Coralville immediately." Her viper eyes drilled into mine. She advanced down a step toward me.

"Ma'am, I'd prefer to wait…" I stammered.

"That is not an option," DeSteele snapped. She grabbed my elbow just as I was attempting to pull out my aerosol. Then she put her face in mine. "And I want the data files on your project turned over to me immediately," she snarled. I felt the aerosol in my purse. She put a vise-like grip on my arm and shook me. I lost hold of the aerosol in the jumble in my purse, then I got it again and managed to get my hand out of my purse while she still had my arm. She turned her attention to the front entrance for a second, then back to me. I wrenched my arm free, put the aerosol to her face, and gave it a hard squeeze.

Startled, DeSteele let go of my arm and stepped back one step. I twisted away from her and ducked through the crowd, but DeSteele was right behind me. "You stop right now!" she screamed at me. People drew back. I got to the sidewalk and tried to blend in with the flow of students. Fortunately everyone's attention was on DeSteele. I moved as quickly as I could down the sidewalk, ignoring the commotion behind me. I got to Rick's Dodge before I risked a look back. Leah was just coming out of the crowd, and behind her, at the front entrance to the building, I saw a jabbering crowd of people and what might have been a figure lying on the steps.

Leah pushed me into the car and we sped away.

"Did you spray her?" Rick asked.

"Yes," I said.

"She went crazy!" Leah gasped, her face white. "She turned on you! You could have been hurt."

"What happened?" Rick asked as he turned onto Second Avenue.

My heart was pounding so hard the words tumbled out in a long stream. "DeSteele was already about to go into the building when I caught up with her. I had planned to catch up with her while she was still on the sidewalk. I was planning to approach her, get her to pause while I asked her about my grant, then pretend to take nasal spray and spray some toward her. She might not even be aware she had gotten…."

Leah interrupted my babble. "DeSteele went crazy. She grabbed Fran by the arm and was waving for someone to…I don't know…I saw Fran bolt down the steps and I followed. I think DeSteele may have fallen down or something."

Back at Rick's apartment I sprawled on the sofa. Rick brought glasses of water, but my hands were shaking so hard I couldn't drink mine.

"You two should stay here tonight," Rick said. "I don't think you should go home until we find out if DeSteele changes or not."

"If anyone's hungry I can order pizza," Rick said. Both Leah and I shook our heads.

"All I want is some sleep," Leah said. "If you've got a pillow I can sleep on this couch."

Rick got out a pillow, a sheet, and a blanket for Leah; then he and I retired to his bedroom. We undressed and got into bed but it was clear neither one of us felt like making love. Rick stroked my hair and my back the way I liked. "I've still got to get my film submitted tomorrow," he said softly. "But I know I can do it. I've got my confidence back and I can ignore the interference from the CI people for a day. It won't be my best work but it will be done."

"I'm sure it will be good." I mumbled from the edge of sleep. I pushed away the knowledge that this might be our last night together, but tears still came to my eyes. I sobbed silently for a time. Rick held me close but said nothing.

Eventually sleep came.

The next morning we were all up early but said little. Rick drove Leah to her car and then took me to my car.

"I'll call you later today," he said.

I could think of nothing more to say, not here on a breezy summer morning. I nodded, kissed him, and drove myself back to my apartment.

I'd just gotten there when my phone pinged. It was an automated text on the UI student network. I was about to delete it when I saw the word "DeSteele."

I opened the message. *We regret to inform our research staff and graduate student researchers that Director of Research DeSteele suffered a stroke and will be out of the office indefinitely. Deputy Director Allenton will be acting director in the interim.*

A cloud of dread began to form in my mind. I went into the bathroom and closed the door and dug into my purse and pulled out the two aerosols.

My worst fears were realized: the aerosol labeled "modulator" still had fluid in it, but the aerosol labeled "deplaquer without mod" was empty.

I set the two little white containers on the counter and looked at my face in the mirror. A great surge of sorrow and guilt rose up in me. I buried my face in my hands and sobbed. *I sprayed her with the wrong aerosol. The stroke she suffered was caused by my deplaquer. I ruined her life.*

Chapter Twelve

The next morning I sat in my apartment living room, staring at the treetops of Iowa City in their lush summertime foliage. Usually this view, in early morning, is among my favorites, but I was exhausted and could only sip coffee and stare unseeing at the beauty of the view. The shaded sidewalks, the trees swaying in the breeze, students walking to and from campus did not cheer me.

I caused DeSteele to have a stroke, but I can never tell anyone about it.

The doctors would not be able to tell that her stroke was induced by inhaling my unmodulated deplaquer. Only a very specialized chemical analysis of her blood would detect it, and they had no reason to order such an analysis.

Earlier I had forced myself to check news sources to see if anyone was suspected of foul play in DeSteele's stroke. There was nothing. My secret appeared to be safe.

If I confess my secret I could be charged with manslaughter, and Rick and Leah would be accomplices. I can't do that to them.

I tried to tell myself that stopping DeSteele's collaboration with Chinese spies justified what I had done, but my conscience was not soothed. I had never intended to hurt her, but my actions had done her great harm. It had been a mistake, a tragic mistake, but there was nothing I could do now to change it.

But what I could do was respond to the invitation from the genetic engineering ethics group at Harvard that had been sitting in my email inbox for two weeks. I would join the group. It would be good to talk with other genetic engineering people about ethical questions.

I texted Leah and told her I was all right, even though I was far from feeling all right. I told her I was still exhausted and was going to try to sleep some more.

She texted: *You shouldn't have to worry about Chinese spies trying to get into your lab. I just heard that the acting director of research has asked the FBI to investigate information flowing from UI research into the Confucius Institute. I'm at my office and I see the CI people are already starting to pack up and move out, which suits me perfectly. I'll talk to you later.*

There was a text from Rick saying he planned to have his project done by three that afternoon. We agreed to meet at the Airliner at four.

He was there at our usual booth when I walked in. There was a cold beer waiting for me. Oldies played on the PA. He did not immediately start talking about film the way he usually does. He seemed as subdued as I felt. I tried not to think that this might be the last time we'd meet here.

Finally he said, "This last week has taught me a lot about how to manage people. Not DeSteele's autocratic way, but by setting goals for people, then letting them find ways to accomplish them. Things are best when all of us keep our clarity, listen to our own minds and hearts. Maybe it's called conscience, I don't know." He touched my hand on the tabletop. "Sorry to ramble on like this."

Conscience. I held back a sob and took his hand in mine. "Yes," I managed to whisper.

He picked up his glass, then set it back down. "Remember our first date? We went to see the movie *Blow-up*."

I remembered it very well. How happy I had been, how simple things seemed then.

"I think of that movie, about confusing reality with illusion, and I think of who I've been in the last few days and it all feels like an illusion." He forced a smile and picked up my hand and kissed it. "I'm really glad I'd already been accepted into USC before my thesis film was posted. It was way too propaganda-ish. I can make better films than that. I was on edge, angry; I was hard on people I shouldn't have been. Hard on you. I'm sorry about that."

"It's okay, Rick."

Rick frowned. "Dr. DeSteele…I heard her stroke is so severe she won't be coming back. I wouldn't wish that on anyone, but at the same time I'm glad she's gone. I don't know if we need to do anything about all the others she poisoned with that stuff you identified. It dissipates naturally over time, doesn't it?"

I said nothing.

"She…" Rick stopped talking but kept fingering his beer glass in a way that I knew meant he was nervous. "But I don't want to talk about her, I want to talk about us. I mean, I do and I don't."

My heart started pounding. I decided to preempt him. "Yes, I want to talk about us too. I really think a lot of you, Rick…" The word love was on the tip of my tongue, but I held it back. Instead I forced myself to say, "I think at this point in our lives, we both need freedom to really focus on our work. Our time together has been wonderful, but…I don't think we can continue." I couldn't say any more.

He smiled softly. "You're a mind reader, Francesca, as well as being smart and beautiful. What you said is exactly what I wanted to say. But I also didn't want to say it." He took both of my hands in his. "You are right—we're good together, but it's too early in our lives to...be together full time, forever."

"Yes," I managed to say in a shaky voice.

Rick breathed a sigh. "I've been really nervous about this. It's hard, but I think it's best. I'm driving back to Chicago tomorrow. I'll spend a few days with my parents, then I'm on my way to Los Angeles."

I tried to smile through my tears and tell him he'd be the next Steven Spielberg, but my voice failed me.

He took my hand and gently pulled me to my feet and we walked out the door arm in arm. There was a nice breeze under the elms that lined Parker Street. We could still hear the oldies playing softly inside. Something about "...go on and kiss him... goodbye..."

And so I did.

Eventually he pulled back and walked away, pausing once to wave.

I made it to my car and sat there letting the tears flow. After a while I dried my face and phoned Leah.

"How about some dinner?"

"Meet at the Airliner?"

"No!" I snapped. I couldn't bear going back into the place where I'd just seen Rick for the last time. "Meet me at the corner of the quad and let's walk to Campus Shoppes and eat dinner there."

Leah was waiting at the corner when I got there. She said nothing about my red eyes. The evening breeze was delicious. I've always liked early summer evenings in Iowa City. The beautiful campus, the trees and the grass of the quad glowed in the gold light. That is what makes academia attractive. This setting and the sense of learning for the pure joy of it.

We got our food and took a window seat with a view of the quad.

Leah studied her vegetable wrap for a moment. "I hate to bring this up, but I am very curious…so…"

"You want to know about Rick and me, right?"

Leah nodded. "Yeah. It's none of my business, I know, but I have really been dreading the moment you tell me that you are going to drop everything and follow Rick to LA, leaving me behind."

"No," I said wistfully, "I'm not going with him." I stabbed a piece of lettuce and studied it. "Rick and I think a lot of each other, but his film work is important to him, and my research is important to me. And we are both too young to face the stresses of being a two-career couple." I felt a lump rise in my throat and stopped talking for a moment. "Rick told me he'd learned a lot about himself recently. So have I. Much as I hate it, this is for the best."

"Here's something else that's for the best," Leah said. "The Confucius Institute is definitely moving out. Some of the corporate interests that fund confidential research up at Coralville got wind of the fact that supposedly secret info was flowing into the CI. They told University Administration to get rid of the CI or they would take their funds elsewhere. When corporate money talks, the university listens."

I felt relieved, but my heart still sagged under its load of guilt. I wanted more than anything to tell Leah what had really happened with DeSteele, but I knew it would just make matters worse.

"Maybe now I'll get an office to myself," Leah said with a grin. "Hey, I'm telling you good news and you look like it's all bad news. Come on, smile."

I tried to.

"You've been under a real strain lately, with Rick leaving and all this stuff with DeSteele. Painful subjects, both of them, so I'll stop talking about them."

Tears welled up in my eyes again, but I managed to say, "Yes, let's forget about them for a while."

My phone chimed. It was a text from my mother, which I read and showed to Leah. She raised her eyebrows. "So…they want you to come home for few days between semesters. Are you going to go, or will you hole up again in your monk-like cell, working on your potions?"

My smile this time was a little bit better. "I need a break. Then I'll go back to my monk-like work habits. I need to get a progress report to my committee, then order more enzyme, then…"

Leah held up her hand. "I don't need to hear your progress report. You are the most organized person I know, Fran. I wish I had your work habits."

"In my report I plan to give Susan the credit she deserves." I stopped short of telling Leah that I planned to synthesize some more modulator as soon as I could and get it to Susan, and somehow get it to others still affected by the half edit. Instead I told Leah, "In answer to your question, yes, I do plan to drive up to Chicago for a few days to visit my parents. Unlike some, I'm a daughter who likes and respects her parents and enjoys their company. Most of the time. For short visits."

Leah patted my hand. "I know you are a dutiful daughter. That's another thing I like about you."

"Say," I said, brightening. "Why don't you come with me? My parents have told me many times they'd like to have you come for a visit. It would be fun."

Leah picked up her phone and checked her calendar. "Well, I've got no plans for the semester break, but I need to prepare for my summer classes. Could we leave Thursday morning and return Sunday morning? That way we miss traffic and I'll have Sunday afternoon to prepare for Monday's classes...can we take your car?"

"Yes, I'll drive. And that's one thing I like about you," I told her. "You make up your mind quickly. I'll pick you up at eight Thursday morning."

"Will I need to take dressy clothes?" Leah asked.

"They'll want us to all go to an opera again," I warned her. "They always do, and I don't want to disappoint them. The Lyric Opera House is quite nice, remember? The food and drink are great, and I'm kind of starting to like opera music. It grows on you. We can dress up a little, which is fun too."

"I'll take a dress…"

"Not your little black dress," I told her. "You look smashing in it, but a little on the hookerish side for my parents."

"Got it. A dressy but conservative dress, don't look or act hookerish, and try to enjoy a four-hour opera I will probably have only marginal interest in."

"That's right," I told her.

She laughed, which started me laughing.

It was great to be alive.